Snickers, the Preacher Cat.

Pollee Freier

iUniverse, Inc.
New York   Bloomington

Snickers, the Preacher Cat.

iUniverse books may be ordered through booksellers or by contacting:

iUniverse
1663 Liberty Drive
Bloomington, IN 47403
www.iuniverse.com
1-800-Authors (1-800-288-4677)

ISBN: 978-1-4401-8000-2 (sc)
ISBN: 978-1-4401-8001-9 (ebk)

Printed in the United States of America

iUniverse rev. date: 11/24/2009

In memory of Merritt D. Freier

Contents

Chapter 1   In the Beginning 1

Chapter 2   What I Have Learned at my Mother's
             Haunch 10

Chapter 3   A Sad Occurrence. 16

Chapter 4   Summertime and the Living Is Easy . . . 20

Chapter 5   The Chipmunk Caper 26

Chapter 6   A Catnapping. 32

Chapter 7   The Boys 38

Chapter 8   The Canine Conundrum 45

Chapter 9   Left to My Own Devices 49

Chapter 10   A Near-Death Experience. 54

Chapter 11   The Care and Keeping of a Vet 61

Chapter 12   Rebellion In the Ranks. 65

Chapter 13   A Murder on the Patio 72

Chapter 14   A Space of My Own. 76

Chapter 15   All Good Things Must Come to an End 80

Epilogue 88

Chapter 1

In the Beginning...

Do you ever wonder what your Cat is thinking? Do you wonder what is going on in that great mind? Is it worth a few hours of your time to find out? If so, you have found the right book, dear reader.

Important things are happening in the intellectual world. For the first time in recorded history, you can be privileged to know what goes on in your Cat's mind. You see, because I can read, I have been able to write down how to please a Cat.

Cats are intelligent, as you have probably ascertained, but we have no way of telling you verbally our wants and needs. However, due to my great mind, and the circumstances in which I found myself, I was able to teach myself to read. You may have determined that already, since I have to be able to read in order to write-a simple deduction.

Now, I may not have been the first Cat to learn to read, but I believe I am the first Cat to write a guide for Cat aides and staffers, to show them the inner workings of a Cat's mind-mine! I can imagine how thrilled you must be, dear reader, to know that you can finally be able to serve your Cat properly.

We Cats are a fascinating bunch. As Sir Walter Scott once opined, "Cats are a mysterious kind of folk. There is more passing in their minds than we are aware of." What a smart man Sir Walter Scott must have been.

Had I not been able to teach myself to read, I never could have written this book. I have prepared this easy to understand manual on how to raise and live with a contented Cat, which I assume is your greatest desire. You will find this is time well spent, for it will make your house run more smoothly.

In a way, I owe my ability to write to the computer, specifically, Pollee's computer. She is one of my aides. She has no idea what I am doing since I work at night while she is asleep. Because of this, I nap a lot during the day.

Merritt and Pollee wanted me to come and live with them, so I gave them a trial run to see if I would be happy in their home. This is customary with Cats although many folks don't know this.

They were an older couple, and he had been a preacher before retiring. They seemed to appreciate me and they were both easily handled; not too bright, humble, and they meant well. They passed the test. They were smart to get a female Cat, because we are better at running a house than males.

So, at the age of three, after a youth of ups and downs, which I won't go into, I found myself living in the home of Merritt and Pollee. It was an old house with three floors, counting the basement. Old houses are always a lot of work because they have entrances for the dratted pest-mice. And mice are common because, generally speaking, old homes that have mice live next to other old homes.

I took my duties very seriously and found I was overworked, but they seemed to appreciate me and were both easily handled by a clever Cat such as me. I am well-organized and experienced, so I was able to take care of the whole house, and I had Pollee and Merritt do my bidding. It took me no time at all to put them in their proper place and they became my faithful servants. This is important if you are a Cat.

Merritt spent a great deal of time holding a leather book in his lap. What he was doing was reading it. Pollee held sticks in her hands and fiddled with yarn. That is called knitting and she made things. She read a lot, too. I had not encountered this sort of thing before, but because of my great intellect and the many books left lying about open, I was able to teach myself to read. I was hampered in my lessons, finding books very hard to open. Cats do not have opposable thumbs, or with them we could rule the world! But that is another story.

Merritt had his books scattered all over the house. Pollee never could make him pick them up. But this failing led to a lot of books being open which helped me in my studies. I must admit that another help was this family's habit of reading to each other.

"Hey, listen to this," one of them would say. And I listened and then would find a way to look at the words myself. I also found that I could sit on the back of the chair they were sitting in and read along with them. My brilliant mind took it in and in no time at all, I was reading.

But the thing that helped me the most was the Bible Study they had in their house. With the meeting in their home, I could look on as they read and also hear them discussing what it said. They never caught on to what I was doing.

Of course, I had to limit my reading to what was in the house. I spent a whole day trying to read a knitting pattern before I realized what it was. What a disappointment. But I was learning all the time.

I was able to read an open book and the one that lay open the most often was this Leather Book. Both Merritt and Pollee seemed to set great store by these Leather Books, and they were all over the house. The same book, different copies. One day, I happened to be standing on the Leather Book.

Merritt said, "Snickers is standing on the Word."

What did this mean? They seemed to think that standing on that book was "cute" on my part. I had stood on other books and they didn't think that was cute, so what was the difference? Later, I found out that the "Word" meant to them the Word of God.

Sometimes we Cats have to do things that seem pointless to our fine minds, but our aides think they are "cute," so a wise Cat will oblige by doing "cute" things to take their little minds off the outrageous things we do. Standing on the Leather Book was one of these things.

You can see where I'm going. The Leather Book was the most prominent book in the house and the one I read the most. I was amazed to read about Jesus. I'm sure He must have had a Cat, or maybe several. One day as I read, I realized that I could be saved, too, so my preaching is to other Cats to tell them the Good News.

My success has been limited, I must admit. But on Sundays, I am a circuit rider, preaching where I can. I can't go too far. I know that roaming around is dangerous, and furthermore, nice Cats don't do that. My mother told us it was the sign of a foolish and wanton Cat, and something else about looking for trouble. I haven't had much success as yet with my preaching, but I am learning. More about that later.

The only thing I could see that would disturb this serene setting was their extended family with young children, always a bad sign. I found that their son, also named Merritt, had a wife, Corrine, and they had three children. The oldest was Hannah, who was away at college most of the time. The two younger children, Emily and Abby, were still at home. These children seemed to think they could pet me, pick me up, and generally bother me. I set them straight. On the bright side, they didn't live with my aides.

Things were going rather smoothly in this house, but suddenly, there was talk of moving, whatever that was. I then noted that Pollee seemed to be collecting cardboard boxes. Now I like boxes. Boxes are fun. I get into them sometimes, because it seems safe there. But Pollee wasn't getting in them; she was collecting boxes from the liquor store, saying that they were the best.

I had never seen either of them drink an alcoholic beverage. I have heard about secret drinkers, so I watched them carefully. They really weren't devious people and I could see that they weren't drinking. A pet doesn't want to get mixed up with heavy drinkers. People under the influence are too unpredictable and apt to be neglectful of a pet's needs, not to mention a pet's wants. Basically, we lose influence with them when they are drinking to excess. So, why the boxes from the liquor store? I soon found out. She was packing all their books in boxes because they said they were moving and the liquor boxes were sturdier. She certainly was moving around more than usual and working hard. Was that what moving was?

Next thing I knew, Mollie was home and I found out that she had her own bedroom. She came home often, I guess. Now Mollie is the daughter and a Cat lover and she was glad when I came into the house, but she has a major flaw. She has an older lady Cat called Ava. Because of Ava's age, I tried to get along, but it was hopeless. She wouldn't fall in line. She claimed she had squatters' rights in my house, and she was to be in charge.

This was unheard of. I was the resident Cat, and it is the rule of the Cats that the resident Cat is in charge. She claimed that she had had the family first, but through Mollie. Ava had visited and knew the house ways. This was true, so I consulted a clever Tabby attorney but he was overruled by a Siamese. They are so shifty-Siamese Cats.

To get back to my story: Mollie grabbed me, which is insulting to begin with, and put Ava and me in her car and took us to another house. I feared we were being Catnapped, but Ava told me we were moving. She had had this happen many times before. Ava is inclined to taunt me, so at first I thought she was making this up. I really didn't know what "moving" meant, but I was soon to learn what it was, and that she had told the truth, for once.

At the end of this disruptive day, we were released from the room we had been put into, for our own good

Mollie said, only to find that we were in a different house! The furniture was the same and Merritt and Pollee were there. They looked a little bedraggled and tired, I might add. They are too old to be doing this sort of thing, was what I thought.

Mollie had only come home to supervise the move and fortunately, she and Ava left. Well, the food was there, so I settled in. A wise Cat realizes that some things are uncontrollable.

I soon found that this was a move for the better as far as I was concerned. And let's face it, that is the only important thing. A Cat's comfort is foremost. If the family Cat is happy, everything will fall in line. Mollie said a smart thing, which was unusual I thought, but I was glad she pointed it out.

"Snickers looks really good in the living room. These are her colors. The brown tones bring out the beauty of her coat to perfection."

It was clever of her to see this and I do set an attractive tone in the room. I also have gorgeous green eyes. Or so I am told. I really am quite modest and don't generally bring up things like this.

As I mentioned before, Ava is a difficult Cat. I have always tried to get along with everyone. I only hiss and bat with my front paws to teach and correct. And I never scratch. Well, to be honest I don't have any front claws. An accident when I was a baby, mother said. But Ava is old and set in her ways. She is nineteen right now. It almost seems vulgar to me for a Cat to live that long, but she is pretty spry. Of course, I might feel different when I am nineteen.

Ava is also very spoiled. She and Mollie live alone and I must admit she has trained Mollie well. Ava goes out of her way to put on airs with me. She has told me repeatedly that she is descended from royal Siamese blood on her mother's side. She says her mother is from "old money." Well, that may be, but she has no right to treat me the way she does in my own home and on my own territory. However, due to my good breeding, I ignore her.

It may seem to some people that I am hissing a lot, but that is a condition with my breathing. I can't help it. Mollie accuses me of hissing absentmindedly, as she puts it. Well, I probably do. I have a lot on my mind as well as a lot to do. I admit it is fun to chide certain people. I have Hannah thoroughly cowed, as she should be. She is a dog lover, you know. A strange person. But the names she calls me and the stories she tells about feeding me are greatly exaggerated. I have never even bitten her. Well, maybe just a nip.

Now the son, also called Merritt, is a fine figure of a man and I like him. He reminds me of Merritt, his father. I like men better, anyway. I try to make up to Merritt, the younger. I rub my beautiful fur on his leg. But, alas, he doesn't seem to like me. No, he must like me. Everyone does. He may be shy, but I will win him over.

Living in the new house is much easier. It is a newer home and has no mice. I make sure of that! There are no mice in this house and never will be as long as I am here. My mousing abilities are well known. So that is one reason my job is easier. I also only have two floors to patrol.

Merritt was always kind to me, but he could only be trained so much and then he had to feel he was getting his own way. But he made a good worker. Of course, Pollee fed me so she had to be kept on a shorter leash, so to speak. She's really a good sort and quite pliable. Ava says she spoils me, but look who's talking! Ava is an example of how far some Cats will go to get their own way with their workers.

I like peace and quiet and a well-run household, and I am proud to say that I run a pretty tight ship. That's one reason I like living here. I can concentrate all my teaching on Pollee and Merritt, and they are quite obedient, for as old as they are.

Chapter 2

What I Have Learned at my Mother's Haunch

The older I get, and I am much older than I look, I find that my mother was the source of all of the important things I ever learned. Most people think that Cats are only nursing when they are at their Mother's side, but they are really learning all they need to know to get along in life.

For example, my mother told us what to expect when we were taken into a home. She stressed that we had to establish dominance at once, because the job would be more difficult the longer we waited. So, while we were yet kittens, we had to very cleverly act cute and still have a firm paw with them, the humans.

We also had to remember that we needed to overcome the bad things we did, in our kittenly ways. You can imagine that this was a tough job. No wonder kittens are so cute and hard to resist. If we weren't, we would be returned, or worse yet, abandoned. That is a terrible thing to do.

I personally have witnessed human babies in homes and believe me, they have to be really cute until they are about 21, or maybe longer. They do some really bad things, like not studying in school, being sassy, not obeying their parents, and worst of all, not being clean like we Cats are. We Cats are much tidier and cleaner than a lot of children. Of course, we do tear things up and sharpen our claws on the wrong things, but really, we make up for it by taking care of our staff. And that is a wonderful thing, being watched after by a Cat.

I probably also learned a lot more than the average Cat because my dear Catly mother, at whose haunch I rested to eat, was a history and literature buff and she knew all about Cats in literature. I'm not going to tell some tall tale about Cats saving the country or some other nonsense that can't be proven one way or the other, but my mother was a lover of good literature and she told us of the heroics of *Puss in Boots*, who was a noble Cat if there ever was one. He made his master, who was a nobody, a Prince. He was a very clever Cat.

Another wise Cat belonged to Dick Whittington. This Cat made Dick the Mayor of London, and it was all through his expertise at ridding areas of mice. These are Cats in fiction, but it gives us real Cats something to aspire to. There was also Jean de la Fontaine, from France. He wrote about a clever Cat who acted as a judge many times. He always benefited from his decisions, I might add.

I have had the advantage of being reared by a literary Cat. Although my mother could not read, she learned most of her stories from listening when the children in her home were read to. She did not have the advantages that I have had. If Merritt and Pollee had closed the Leather Book when they were through with it, and been tidier in closing and putting books away, I would never have been able to teach myself to read. I am grateful they were the way they were, messy.

Has it ever occurred to you that we Cats have given the mouse a lot of free publicity? Where would the mouse be today without the Cat? And not all the publicity they have gotten from or through us has been bad. Some people actually feel sorry for the mouse! Look at the cartoon "Jer and Tommy," or whatever it is called. It is a piece of wily propaganda that has poisoned the minds of innocent children against us, the noble Cat.

Cats are on the side of right, and cleanliness and all those good things. In these cartoons, the poor mouse is always badgered by a bully Cat. It's grossly unfair, but it is the way of life, my mother always said. We get the thrill of the chase, and it is nice to be better at something than anybody else is.

My mother taught us the proper and best way to hunt out and kill the vermin-mice, pesky things. She left nothing to chance. She taught us everything we needed to know about it. I would have liked to share my hunting expertise with Merritt. He was a hunter, but we had no way to communicate. I know he would have appreciated my thoughts on the subject.

I don't know how my dear mother accomplished all she did in such a short time. Of course, it occurs to me that we were unusually bright kittens and caught on fast. And we had inherited good hunting skills, too.

I came from a litter of three kits, all females. We had a wonderful kittenhood, but we all learned at our mother's haunch as we were nursing. Mother showed us how to act "cute" when the future owners came to look at us. And we had a natural talent for looking attractive. We were all picked quickly, and I was the first to go. Of course, we didn't go until mother was satisfied that we had learned all we needed to know.

She spent a lot of time teaching us girls about being mothers. She said it was a great thing to have happen: to be a mother, or a queen, as she called a mother Cat. The problem is, I have never become a Mother. I don't know why. I know that there was a time when I thought that Toms were rather attractive and exciting. But then I lost that feeling. I have heard it said that when we Cats go to the vets and stay awhile, with a lot of pleasant dreaming time, something happens. But what? And why? Well, no matter. I know how to raise a kitten if I have to. But it is puzzling.

While I am on the subject of learning and teaching, I want to say that I have had a hard enough time writing this treatise, what with no thumbs, getting up at 2:00 a.m. to write and then having my creative juices dry up, and one thing or another. Now, I hear that someone has criticized my writing style. They said, "Don't end a sentence with a proposition."

Well, I have never propositioned anyone in my life. As a matter of fact, I have never been propositioned myself. After all my mother told us about Toms, I would have sent one packing if I were propositioned by one of them. So to be accused of ending a sentence with a proposition is something I have never thought of. What kind of Cat do people think I am?

AVA

As most of you know, Ava has gone to her reward, at the ripe old age of 19, of natural causes. Now I feel terrible for criticizing her. I know I was rather harsh, and I want to correct, or tone down, some things I said. Yes, Ava was a bossy Cat. But on thinking over what I wrote about her wanting to be the head Cat when she was here, I realize she had been with Pollee and Merritt before I was, and that does mean something. I'm not saying that I wasn't right, but I could have been kinder, perhaps, than I was.

Some people who know me find it amazing that I am, in a way, admitting that I might have made a mistake. "To err is human," as Alexander Pope once said, but Ava may have had a point about prior commitment to Pollee and Merritt. They knew Ava, and maybe seeing how much pleasure she gave Mollie did influence their decision to get a Cat. Not all people are as open minded about having a Cat as they were, after having had dogs all their lives.

I want to go on record as saying that although Ava deliberately teased and taunted me in front of everyone, I still should have "turned the other cheek." She did this teasing in such a way that made me look bad to my owners. It was as though I was being unkind to her, when I was really cowering.

Well, at this time, I had not read the Leather Book. In fact, I couldn't even read. I thought I had to be firm with her. That is generally the best way, but maybe I was too harsh. And I must admit, I have never seen an owner better trained than Mollie. Ava did a wonderful job molding and shaping her to the Cat's way of thinking.

She was even a bit brainwashed, I thought, which blinded her to some of my exceptional qualities.

I think that in the last few months, Mollie has softened toward me. And that alone is an amazing thing. She is getting older, and maybe she is mellowing. I hope she finds a Cat who will take the time and patience that Ava did in her training. It is beautiful to see how a Cat can train a person to almost think like a Cat, and any Cat Mollie brings into her home will benefit from Ava's teaching. That is a *great tribute* to a Cat.

Chapter 3

A Sad Occurrence

I'm sorry to have to report another death in the family. Much closer to home, so to speak. Although it wasn't unexpected, Merritt, my friend and helper, has died. He had been very sick for awhile, so it wasn't a surprise, but Pollee says death is always a surprise. Merritt was always so nice to me, and I might add, to everyone else, too. Pollee is sad and cries, but she knows where he went. She knows he is in Heaven and happy not to be sick. Being sick is not good. But Pollee misses him, even though she knows he was very sick and ready to go.

This means that I have had to really work hard to comfort her. That's probably why I came to this house, although I thought at the time that I had picked them out. I think Jesus sent me here. And I am certainly glad that He did.

Pollee relies on me more now by talking to me a lot. That is good. I listen carefully, so that I can find out how to help her. This is a new experience for me. I am the one who is supposed to be taken care of. Well, I will step in and try to be a bother to take her mind off her loss. That's the best thing to do. And I will continue to write about how I learned to read because Merritt left his books lying around, especially the Leather Book.

It has just occurred to me that, you, dear reader, may want to know more about what sort of Cat I am. First of all, I am eight years old, a good age for a Cat, not too old but mature enough to have great wisdom. Although I look heavy, I am only about 12 pounds, all muscle. The vet expects me to lose 2 pounds. I say that's ridiculous.

Ava always bragged about the Siamese connection, poor dear, but I have good blood in me, too. I am a Manx. That should be enough to tell you a lot, but I know that the common person is not always as well informed about Cats as a Cat might wish.

The Manx was first found on the Isle of Man, which is off the coast of England in the Irish Sea. Some people think that we came from ships that sank; maybe some from the Spanish Armada, when they came to try to conquer England. We Cats have always been valued on ships for our excellent mousing skills, one of our many talents. So, the Manx probably were in a shipwreck and swam from a ship of some sort to the Isle of Man. The language on the Isle of Man is called Manx so that may be why we are called Manx. My immediate family came from Missouri and is highly respected.

Of course, we Manx are readily recognized because we don't need tails. There has been much conversation regarding the importance of a Cat's tail. It is all false. It is an absolutely useless appendage. It's value is highly touted, but no Cat "needs" a tail. Just look at the Manx. We can do anything any other Cat can do, and generally better, without a tail.

I digress to give some examples of the rude questions that I get from imbeciles because I am a Manx, such as "Where's your tail?" or "Someone must have cut her tail off." or "That Cat doesn't have a tail!"

The ignorance of the commoner is abysmal. But what can I say? They know not what they do. I "turn the other cheek." I learned that from the Leather Book.

Besides having the distinction of being a Manx, I also have a beautiful orange, brown, white and black coat, referred to as calico. Because of my beautiful appearance, people often make overtures to me. I do not welcome strangers coming up to me and trying to pet me, especially after making rude remarks about my appearance. This may make me appear unpleasant. I am a friendly Cat, however, I will make the first move.

I am always interested in seeing who comes into the house. I go to the door with Pollee. Isn't that being friendly? I feel that I should help keep an eye on who my person consorts with. After all, she is alone now. But she is very casual about screening people who come in. I say, you can't be too careful. The silverware and other valuables may be in danger. I am only sorry that people won't leave me alone. So it isn't my fault if people are hissed at. You can understand that, I'm sure.

If you could hear the sweet dulcet tones of my beautiful voice, you would know that I am adorable and harmless. Merritt used to say that I had a piteous mew, but I prefer to think of it as sweetly reminding Pollee that she has forgotten to do something for me. I don't like to see her fall down on the job. She is usually quite attentive, but even the best aides forget sometimes. I just don't want it to happen often. There is a limit to what a Cat should have to put up with.

Speaking of voices, Ava had a raucous whiskey baritone. I think it is very unbecoming for a lady Cat. Mollie said it was the Siamese in her. I don't doubt it. I've heard they are pretty heavy drinkers.

Another comparison that had been made between Ava and me is our weight. I don't understand this obsession with weight these days. As I mentioned, my doctor, another member of my staff, thinks I need to lose weight. How absurd! I am a fine figure of a Cat. This is my best weight. But to call me obese? I bit him a few times and he hasn't said that again. The injustice of it all! I am big-boned. I admit freely to this, but I carefully watch what I eat. Some people do make remarks about my figure. I think that is an ill-bred thing to do. Why, just last night some man said, "Pollee, that Cat is fat."

He said this after a rude comment about my absence of a tail.. No wonder I'm crabby today.

I hope that you don't think I was jealous of Ava, that scrawny thing! She was told she needed to gain weight. I should think so. Mollie said that Ava was her panther Cat. What a silly comparison. Just because she was black. That's a bad thing, if you ask me. I could tell you stories about black Cats and bad luck that would make your hair curl. Why, I heard once...but I won't go into that. I never gossip. I am too sweet-natured to do that, and the Leather Book says Christians shouldn't do that. So I don't.

Chapter 4

Summertime and the Living Is Easy

"Summertime and the living is easy" is a line from a song that Pollee sings a lot. She must get an ear worm. You know, an ear worm is when the same song runs through your mind all day and drives you nuts. I learned that name from Pollee's grandchildren. I like to keep up-to-date on things. But to get back to my story, sometimes she will sing the same song all day, like "Summertime." I try to ignore the lyrics to that song, but the words do annoy me a bit. I am even-tempered, but hearing those words, "And the living is easy," is upsetting. Living is not easy for a Cat in the summer. For example, the summer brings out all sorts of creatures and they think they can live in my yard.

When we first moved into the house we are in now, I didn't go outdoors. But when I finally discovered the back and front yards, I insisted that I had to look them over. I am sorry to tell you, both yards are full of bad sorts, like chipmunks, squirrels, rabbits and mice, in the woodpile. All a rough lot. And the birds! The place was covered with them because Pollee fed them! Well, not the riffraff;

she just fed the birds. I think it is disgraceful. I keep them away and I believe she has become discouraged about it. But I will not put up with other creatures in my yard.

It is depressing, though. The low-life is so plentiful. I try to patrol our front and back yards and a few yards on either side. I do what I can. But any Cat would tell you that I am busy! And it is a big responsibility. I shoulder the work and find that I am never done. I'm not a complainer, but sometimes I think that I am the only person who tries to keep things up around here.

Some people think that Cats sleep a lot. If they only knew. I am up at all hours...cleaning the house and myself. A Cat can't be too clean. Yes, I keep my things in order, and I have to patrol the whole house. I have to watch the neighborhood, too. I sit on the couch in front of the window and keep an eye on things. I see the Cat across the street doing the same thing. That way, we cover most of the houses.

Although Merritt is gone, I still go down to the basement. I do miss him and the basement reminds me of him, because this was his study. We often spent an afternoon studying together. I would sit on the back of his chair and look over his shoulder. The basement is quite nice, always cool in the summer and has comfortable couches and chairs. Pollee goes down a lot, too. She misses him, but sometimes she goes down to look something up in the encyclopedia. We have several sets. I think it adds a touch of class to the place, myself. The reason we have so many is that Pollee and Merritt worked for a publishing company many years ago. When Pollee looks things up, she often leaves those books open, so it makes for good reading for me, too.

It has been different with Merritt gone. I knew he was not getting better, but he always said he was. He was a good man and he is in a good place, Heaven, and we can only guess what it is like. But we are assured it is better than Earth. Pollee still takes good care of me, though. Maybe better. When there are just two of you, you do tend to take better care of the other one.

I try to help her by being "cute." I feel I should explain that I have a very pleasant disposition, but because of some vertical dark stripes between my eyes, I look stern, with a slight frown or even a judgmental look. Most of the time, I like looking that way. It keeps people at a distance and they don't get too friendly with me. But it is not my nature to those who are my helpers. I really do love Pollee and I loved Merritt before he left, as much as a Cat can love their people. They have been good to me.

One "cute" thing I do is roll on the cement on the patio when it is all warm from the sun. It feels so good on my back. The sun has baked it and it warms my bones. I suppose it isn't very dignified, and I am a dignified Cat, but I do it because she likes to see me do it. I don't do it for myself, of course, but just to make her smile.

She thinks I'm "cute" when I mew softly to have her come in and pet me while I eat. And she generally puts down her book or her knitting and obliges me. I have special ways I look "cute." I peer out at her from under things. Occasionally I will rub her ankles-not too often-and she thinks that's "cute."

Pollee and I have a good sleeping arrangement. After she gets in bed, I jump up on the bed and she speaks to me. I go over to her and she scratches my head. That feels good! Cats have a hard time scratching their heads. I can't really clean it either. So she scratches away. And she doesn't miss my ears. She has a sweater of hers on the bed for me to sleep on.

She does things that baffle and amaze me. I try to be tolerant, but I do let her know I think her behavior is odd. She thinks that's "cute."

Sometimes, I want to jump up to the counter in the bathroom. I do that often, but every once in a while, it seems so high. I know I am getting older. So, I start, then I back up and decide not to do it. She encourages me. I measure the distance by standing on my hind legs. She continues to tell me I can do it. I finally jump and make it with ease. She is always pleased to see me succeed. That's when *I* think *she's* "cute." I also like it when she speaks to me and calls me a "bum." That must mean somebody really wonderful.

I love to sleep or rest on her knitting if she leaves it lying about. The wool is so soft, and it smells of her. I like the way she smells, even when she has been doing her laps in the pool. I think she leaves her just-completed sweaters out for me to sleep on. It is sort of a test run. We are very close. When I am hunting mice in the wood pile and she calls me, I try to come out to see what she wants. However, if I am hunting, I can't always come out.

You see, I am not just hunting when I am out. I am conducting a Scientific Study on the behavior of the strange, and disgusting American Squirrel. I am doing this for my Cat Study Group. You have heard the expression, "curiosity of a Cat"? Well, over time a word has been left out. It should read, "The intellectual curiosity of the Cat." You see the difference? And that is another reason why I am doing this study. I am intellectual.

I have a grant to delve into the behavior of some of the more useless small mammals in America. I have been asked to give a paper on this subject. I got this grant from a rich Cat who had been left a great deal of money. He felt that this was an important topic and he gave me the money. He said that he might as well give it to me, because if the overseers of the estate could, they would kill him and take the money. So sad.

You see, Pollee studies things for her study group. Mollie reads papers for the Pop-Culture group. I think that's what she calls it. Or is it the Culture of Pop? I guess it's Pop-Culture. Anyway, she "reads" papers. I guess this is a group of humans who can't read and want someone to read to them. Sounds strange to me. But Mollie is a philosophical doctor or a "pst" or something. Her associates may be a bit odd.

I do my papers to keep my mind active. With being able to read and coming from a family with a preacher and a "pst" in the family, my friends expect more of me, and I try to oblige. They always hang on every word I say. Occasionally, they yawn, but everyone does that when they are tired.

Sometimes, I think my life is all work and no play, but I feel it is my duty to do these things, since I have this wonderful ability and mind. And can you imagine how pleased my fellow Cats are to have me lecture them?

In case you wonder how I "write" papers, I use the computer. Where would I be without Pollee's computer? I also prepare my sermons on the computer. My typing is slow because I use the "hunt-and-peck" system, of course. Need I remind you again, no thumbs.

Maybe I should stay silent about these activities, but I feel this helps the reader to understand Cats better. And that is always a good thing. We are complex.

Back to my paper on squirrels...such a fascinating topic. I have thought of enlarging my study to include rabbits, but all those bunnies! I would be fortunate to have such a fertile area to study. I could include chipmunks.

There was a family of chipmunks under the patio, but I accidentally exterminated the last family member. Or maybe they're in hiding. I'm glad they are gone either way. I hate them! I know it says in the Leather Book to love our enemies, but do you think that includes such unloveable sorts? I think not! The Lord knows how hard some of these creatures are to love. I know, I know. We are supposed to forgive. But am I supposed to forgive these chipmunks when they have accused me of lying to them? Oh, dear, I'll have to ponder that. I have to do so much of that, my ponderer gets sore. More later after I have solved this problem.

Chapter 5

The Chipmunk Caper

This might be a good time to tell you about The Chipmunk Caper, as I like to call it. It's quite a tale. You will find it hard to believe.

I was downstairs studying and I heard this noise and it was a chipmunk! Right in the house! To say I was surprised is an understatement. I was shocked, dear reader. Where did she come from? What did she have in mind? Was she planning on taking over my basement? I sneaked over to where she was and challenged her, from a distance, I might add. Chipmunks might look small, but in person, they are much bigger, trust me.

She was frightened and disoriented and had no idea where she was. When I told her, she was amazed. All she would say was that she had felt a warm breeze coming from the house and went to investigate. It was a chilly fall day.

I finally concluded that she had fallen into the dryer vent. There must have been a hole in the plastic fitting and she apparently ended up behind the dryer. Later, I heard Pollee tell Merritt there was no hole in the plastic. Very puzzling. The chipmunk was upset and assured me she had no intention of being there. She introduced herself. Her name was Wood and she came from the Chip family. They do have odd names in some of those old families.

I felt sorry for her. Her main goal was to get out of there as quickly as possible. As we were talking, Pollee came down the stairs and sensed that there was trouble in the air. She saw me and knew I was in my hunting stance. She was instantly alert, counting on me to keep anything dangerous away from her. I tried to act nonchalant.

She spied Wood. To distract her, I acted as if I were challenging the varmint. It was a tense moment because Wood had no idea what to do. I cautioned her to remain silent. Pollee wisely turned the situation over to me and went upstairs.

I knew that Pollee didn't want a chipmunk in the house. Neither did I. No telling what would happen because Wood was a wild animal and she had no experience in a person's home. I have seen unsophisticated animals go absolutely crazy in a house.

Wood was very edgy as we talked. We knew that we had to find a way out for her. I didn't tell her that I knew she couldn't climb back up the inside of the dryer vent. I needed time to put my great brain to work and figure something out. We needed to have a plan, but I couldn't imagine what it would be.

After talking the situation over, we finally decided that the best thing to do was for her to settle down and take a little nap. That was my idea. Things always look better when you are rested. Then I would begin training her for her escape. I suggested that she retire to the Gun Room. She climbed into a black sack containing hunting clothes. This sort of thing always smells of the outdoors and she liked it. She settled in and soon I determined that she was resting comfortably.

I felt responsible for the poor dear and pondered her fate. I wouldn't kill her and frankly she was a big robust girl. I might have my hands full. So I tried to think of how she would get out. If I could get them to open a window in the basement, that would solve the problem. But with winter coming on, there was no way they would open a window, and take out the screen, as well.

If it were summer, I could figure a way for my aides to keep an outside door open awhile. I decided that getting them to open the door into the garage would be the best way, although it would involve her climbing the stairs, but everything I could think of would do that. Then I spent a lot of time trying to think of how to get them to open the door into the garage in this cold weather.

I decided that the best way was the Indecisive Game. It works like this. You sit in front of the door, mewing softly. When the staff opens the door to let you out, you act as though you are pondering what to do now that the door is open. You start out, then pause, with the door still open. Then you want to come in, then start out again. This is repeated a few times. When you sense that your people are really exasperated, slip out.

This is an amusing game for Cats and the staff is reminded again who is in charge. While I was distracting them, Wood could slip out. When one of my aides opened the garage door to take the car out, she could seize the moment. It might work, and what else was there?

I admit it took me a few days to think this out. You must have a perfect plan to make sure all will go well. In the meantime, Pollee began walking around the basement, peering and sniffing a lot. At first I thought she had caught a cold, but I finally realized that she was trying to smell any unusual odors, like a dead animal. What could she smell anyway? Humans have no sense of smell. It's those ridiculous noses they have. They are so handicapped, poor dears.

As far as I knew, Wood was still in the plastic sack all this time. I heard nothing from her. I waited for her to come out. The grandchildren came down and played and watched TV. They are noisy, and I thought that Wood would be scared and come out to talk to me. But no sign of her. I finally decided that she had found a way out and left without saying goodbye to me, which I thought was rather rude. But we are not dealing with a cultured animal here.

Well, one day, Pollee was in the Gun Room looking for something and she looked in that bag. Lo and behold, Wood was in there, dead! We were both shocked. There had never been any odor. I had never heard a sound from her. I wanted an autopsy because I knew my reputation was at stake. But, of course, Pollee didn't understand what I was trying to say. She just bundled the body up and threw it out. Sometimes she is heartless, and dimwitted.

Several months later, in the spring, I was out in the yard and saw Wood's family and told them what had happened. They were furious with me. They blamed me for the whole thing! They had some idea that I had lured her into the basement. How foolish. Why would I do that? But they are very simple and couldn't grasp what a basement was, let alone what had happened.

Ever since then, they have hated me. They never thanked me for trying to help Wood. I have often wondered if she was sick and they pushed her down the vent. I wouldn't put it past them. Very backward bunch.

I finally washed my paws of the whole thing. They never believed me. And neither did Ava, Mollie's Cat! She said I was frightened of Wood and told her to go into the bag and then I tied it closed. So, basically, I murdered her. It's hard to think that a friend, a fellow Cat, would think such a thing of me. I admit, the thought had crossed my mind. I knew we would have trouble getting her out. But I didn't do it. I have a very hard time tying things, anyway. It's so hard to be misunderstood all the time.

I turned the other cheek. I read about that in the Leather Book. I also heard that we were to forgive. Well, I'm sure Jesus doesn't expect me to forgive those chipmunks. They were awful to me and called me a liar and a murderer. So, I know that doesn't apply to me. I think that Jesus meant that when someone politely apologizes to you, after awhile, you forgive them. You can probably wait a few days or so and then tell them that all is forgiven, sigh, and smile sadly at them.

I'm not sure you have to forget about it, though. You can subtly bring it up, now and then. Then say, it's in the past, and sigh and smile again. That sounds good to me. This only works if you can get someone to admit they were wrong to begin with, and ask forgiveness.

I do wish Jesus hadn't talked about it so much. I think He even mentioned it when He told us how to pray. Yes, here it is. "Forgive us our debts, trespasses, sins, as we forgive those who sin against us." Hummm. Well, there must be an answer. It's pretty clear, though. I never really noticed that before. I certainly want Jesus to forgive me! Where would I be if He didn't? I'd be in terrible trouble! Let me look in another version. Same thing.

So, what you are telling me, Lord, is that I am supposed to forgive those dratted little chipmunks? I can't! I tried to help them! It was not my fault. Doesn't that count for anything, Lord? And they don't even know You! Surely, You mean that we are just to forgive fellow Christians?

No, it doesn't say anywhere about just forgiving your fellow Christians. You just said forgive. And I remember now that You forgave those awful men who tortured You, and put You to death. Oh, I am undone. I can't do it, Lord. You have to help me! I give up! It's hopeless! I thought I was called and that You wanted me to preach, and everything. I thought I was Your child.

I know it was real when You spoke to me, Lord. So, I guess that means that if I want to continue in Your care, I have to try, at least, to obey You. There is only one way I can do that, Father. You have to take over and do it for me. You have to change my wicked heart.

Lord, I want to wipe the slate clean. I forgive everyone I have anything against. And, Lord, when I feel that bad feeling of unforgiveness coming back, You have to stop me and help me again. And if I still don't, then I won't have my sins forgiven. That thought should scare me into behaving.

You did it, Lord. I don't hate them. I have forgiven them. What a wonderful thing that is! I have never felt so peaceful in my life. This is that same wonderful way I felt when I first got to know You. I hope I can remember this lesson, Lord. But if I don't, I know You will gently remind me.

Chapter 6

A Catnapping

I was terrified at first. They were planning on Catnapping me. But the more I thought about it, why Catnap me? Pollee is not a wealthy person. Yes, I am from a noble line and I can prove it, but only by Cat Lore and tales. I have no papers or proof written down. I am a beautiful Cat, but I am not valuable, monetarily. But I had heard the man say to the woman, "Ready for a Catnap?"

My blood ran cold! They were planning a serious crime in such a nonchalant manner! Did I hear them correctly? Yes, that's what he said. I know how serious a crime Cat or kidnapping is. I know that kidnapping a child is a horrible thing to do. People can be killed for doing that.

I have heard of Cats being Catnapped who won contests. I'm not exactly sure about that. But I know word gets around in Cat circles that this or that champion Cat had been napped or snatched.

I thought it would never happen in this neighborhood. Most of the time, a champion Cat is known about in their area. And I had never heard anything about one here. I put that couple under surveillance. I had other pets watching, too. I told them what I had overheard. They were as shocked as I was.

The suspects had not lived in that house too long. The lady who lived there before, with a yappy dog, was very nice. But she died. So, I kept my eye on this new couple. I knew they had no pets-always a questionable trait, I say. They seemed hard working and were often out in the yard. I allowed them to see me one day and she remarked to him that I was an attractive Cat. He agreed and said that he thought I lived behind them, which was true.

Summer changed to winter, and one night, when I got up to write, I glanced out the patio door and noticed a light on in their window. It was about 2:30 a.m., and time for all respectable people to be in bed. Were they part of a gang, and the gang was meeting in their home? No good can come out of a meeting at this time of night. It looked suspicious.

Pollee doesn't let me out at night. She says bad things can happen to Cats at night. I know this is true because my mother said the same thing. It was impossible for me to get out and see if I could hear anything through the windows.

After watching for several nights, I realized that the light stayed on till morning. Another thing, there was snow on the ground, but no people prints on it. I found this very strange.

As spring approached, I saw them again. They were out in the yard, and that night, I noticed their light wasn't on all night. Maybe they had gone away to Catnap some Cat. After further investigation, I realized that the light went off every night. Also, I detected no pet of any kind around the house. So they weren't holding some innocent Cat for ransom.

I put out an alert again, telling the neighborhood pets that I had an eye on things and would continue to watch the suspects. We have a good neighborhood watch here. We are able to communicate well. This is done, Cat-to-Cat, and often the dogs join in. Dogs are walked by their people and can talk to each other, and they have the Bark, too. I understand Bark pretty well, and that is not saying much. The Bark is a pretty elementary language. Most of the time, it is used for friendly greetings and gossip.

One might say, "Hi there, Spot. All well at your house?" and Spot responds that it is. Or maybe they pass along some harmless gossip. You can almost guess what they are going to say. Most pets can give a pretty good translation of a Bark message. Cats can't speak it because we are not equipped to make that kind of sound.

When we moved here, the presence of a Cat was noted, even though I wasn't going out at that time. In fact, many thought there were two Cats here, because Ava came with Mollie to help Pollee and Merritt move.

I wish Ava were here so that I could talk to her about the Catnappers. Ava used to live in college towns and had an aura of sophistication about her. She was pretty world-wise. It sounds to me like the people in those towns were treated badly.

Ava said there was always a lot of complaining about people not being punished for something like stealing. I think the word was plage-rythm. What do you suppose they stole? If these people were caught, they had to teach Freshman Writing. Surely handwriting was taught to students before they got to college? I wish I could check that out with Ava.

As time went on, I realized that I might be in more danger than I thought from those Catnappers. Although I am not a Champion, or from a wealthy family, I am smart, I have a logical mind, and I can read. If they found this out, they might figure they could use me to spy on people or to be a guest on late night TV shows and <u>they</u> would get all the praise and be paid for <u>my</u> performance.

As for spying, we Cats would do well at that! We are quiet and can be very secretive about where we are. We blend into the background, and even if we don't, no one thinks we know what's going on. There is a saying in the Netherlands. I think that is where it is. "Don't talk in front of your Cat. Cats are gossips." I prefer to think that what they mean is that Cats are very nosy, or inquisitive. A Cat like me would be invaluable to a detective. I could even type up my own reports.

These thoughts galvanized me into action. I found out that the suspects' neighbor had a Cat. She is an attractive gray-and-black striped female. In fact, Pollee saw us consulting in our yard one day. This Cat had given me a report and told me something surprising, and I yowled. Pollee looked out so we pretended to be upset with each other and I chased her home.

Pollee is slow, but sometimes she figures things out. When she saw us, we were not in a typical fighting position; she frowned and looked puzzled. We were being friendly. She wondered about this. So, I would have to be careful.

But the mystery was solved. That Cat told me that a Catnap is a short nap. Last night, I managed to knock the dictionary onto the floor. Fortunately, it fell open and I looked up the meaning and that other Cat was right! How was I to know this? I was shocked. Any Cat with a logical mind like mine would have thought like I did. The English language is strange. All the pets are now accusing me of creating an uproar over nothing. So, I try to keep things safe and sound for everyone and look at the thanks I get!

I found out that these new neighbors go away to the South every winter where it is very warm. They had a mechanism to turn the light on every night. They do this so the burglars will think someone is home. That wouldn't fool me, if I were a burglar.

Going south doesn't appeal to me. I have this great, warm coat, and so beautiful, too. Of course, I couldn't leave Pollee and the neighborhood. I am pretty important around here, although some of the pets don't realize it.... yet!

For awhile I felt pretty stupid, but not for long. I realized that I had accomplished quite a bit. I established a secure neighborhood communication system. We pets cooperated and set up clever security measures, and who knows, it is probably for the best. If we had a Terrorist attack, we would have everything under control.

A second blessing for our staff, or owners, as the dogs would say, is that we can relay messages from one end of the block to the other, and to the adjoining street, as well. The Corgi next door pointed out to me that most owners on this street are pretty long in the tooth, if you know what I mean. I know they like to think they are not, but we must face facts. And, if anything happened to one of them, we could pass the info on. So, I am feeling good about it all.

I know you are saying, for example, how would you get out to tell anyone if Pollee was sick? So I am refining a complicated plan. Each animal who can roam a bit, just a bit, will check with their neighbors through the windows and report that all is well. We could set up a paw signal if there were trouble. Then the dogs can put out a Bark warning.

Sometimes I wonder about Pollee. She never complains about dogs barking. Does she know more than I think? Did she see *One Hundred and One Dalmatians*, and learn about the communication between dogs? On second thought, no, she's not that bright. She can't have figured out that we pets are communicating all of the time. She's pretty aware, but when you come right down to it, she wouldn't know. Never in a million years!

Chapter 7

The Boys

I'm slowly getting my strength back after that troubling, harrowing, and tense weekend with "the boys." I may be able to write about it now. Thinking about it does not upset my stomach or make me tremble anymore. Why Pollee feels she has to have company in this house most of the time, I don't know.

Can't she be content with just the two of us? I am excellent company and that should be more than enough. But she has wanderlust, I think it's called, and nothing will satisfy her inclinations to leave unless it's someone coming in here. But that's the way she is, so I have to try to keep a keen eye on who comes in and out. When she does leave me she has Shirley come in to feed me and Shirley is very good at what she does. I don't mind her at all.

Mollie comes and goes as she pleases and I have gotten used to her. I still clear my throat at her to remind her that I am not changing my attitude. But those adolescent Cats she calls "boys!" First, I would have thought that she would have had a mourning period for Ava. Pollee says she is showing her love for Ava by adopting those adolescents. Well, why didn't she get a dignified Cat? Oh, no, she adopts two five month old kittens, she calls them.

As soon as she let them out of the carrier, I could see that we were in trouble. They stopped to say hello to me and pay their respects and then they were off! They seemed to have the rudiments of good manners, but not for long. They had no hesitation about running anywhere in the house they wished. They tried to eat my food, but Pollee did attempt to stop them from doing that and managed to salvage some for me. They went into every nook and cranny, jumped on Pollee's bed, and she did nothing to stop this rampage. I was afraid they would vandalize the house.

They were big galoots. Domino, ("Dom" for short) has very big feet. And those feet don't just look that way because they are white. They *are* big. That is an obvious sign that a cat will be big when fully grown.

Of course, I was horrified. I did hiss and growl. Yes, I admit that. But they were out of control. Mollie had the good sense to close the door to the lower level. They played with the toys I had left for them. Well, I hadn't actually left them; they dragged them out. And they played with my special Cat scratcher. Pollee has put a little, very little, catnip for me on that. If Darcy has a hangover, it serves him right. It's not the sort of toy a young teen should be playing with anyway. Someone should have stopped him.

They marched in here and took over the house in an instant. They called to me, "Hi, Aunt Snickers!" One said, "I'm Domino!" and the other said, "I'm Darcy!"

Yes, I admit Pollee had told me about "the boys" coming. She spoke as though they were young. She used the word "kitten." Those boys were teenagers! And big ones at that. These "kittens" will be as big as small ponies when they become Toms. I heard Mollie say that, and she was laughing. What is she thinking?

I had visions of them sitting respectfully at my side while I counseled them on life and how to be a good Cat. That's how I behaved when I was a kitten. Pollee immediately picked them up and cuddled them, and they let her. I don't allow such familiarity from her except on special occasions.

She is allowed to pick me up and speak to me, even an occasional pat, but no cuddling, except on my terms, and when I feel like it. And I don't often feel like it. It's too much like letting her have her own way with me. She has to keep her distance. I feel that I am not in control when she does what she wants. I am in charge here. I think I have explained that before.

This new generation of Cats is being trained differently. We kittens were to be tolerated, but today, they are petted and held. This only trains them to be people-friendly. The ads in the *Cat Magazine* brag that the kittens advertised are raised underfoot. This means they are picked up, cuddled, and get used to people. They have no privacy, I say. I can't imagine that. Aides will never learn their place that way.

Well, things went from bad to worse. Pollee had invited Merritt, the younger, and his family over and the whole crew came. The girls, in particular, played with those kittens and the kittens allowed it.

Everyone looked on, smiling and encouraging those Cats. Yes, they were Cats. They were adolescent Toms, not kittens. I would have been more friendly if they had been kittens. After all, I learned from Mother how to raise kittens.

Even Hannah, who said she didn't like Cats because of me, played with them. I keep telling people that it really was more of a simple nip, not a bite, when we had that disagreement. But she doesn't like Cats now, because of that. Corrine joined right in, but I noticed that Merritt didn't. That was the only ray of light through the whole episode.

Well, you know what adolescents are like. They roughhoused right in the living room, they ran about, and they played with the girls. I had no control over them. If I tried to correct them they answered that their mother, Mollie, didn't care if they acted like this. And they were right. She beamed on them as if they were doing something cute!

Well, I could do nothing. They ate, and I growled. They played some more, and I growled. I cleared my throat, which sounds like hissing, and growled. And no one cared. Pollee told me to be nice to them, as if I could have had a chance!

Finally, Merritt and family went home and it was time for bed. Mollie took the Cats into her room and shut the door. That gave me an opportunity to access the damage, quietly patrol the house, and go to bed with Pollee. I felt I should protect her in case "the boys" got out and attacked her. I stayed by her side for most of the night.

By morning, it was clear that they were going to be here while the people went to church. So, I went outside and patrolled. No, I was not pouting as some people said. I was working, as usual. Others may be able to play all the time, but I don't have that privilege. I am a working Cat, that's how they describe Manx in Cat literature. And that's what we Manx's do-work. You know, they say that a Cat's work is never done.

I didn't have a chance to talk to "the boys" about their heritage. Mollie is right; they do look like Ava and, therefore, they must be at least part Siamese. They are litter mates and Darcy is all black, just like Ava. Even though black Cats are said to be bad luck, Mollie pays no attention to that.

Mollie picked them out at the Cat Shelter in Springfield. I have been in the Shelter here in Quincy and they do try to do good works. Being left to take care of oneself is not good for any Cat. And some humans are bad people and don't deserve a Cat, I can tell you that.

These Cats landed on their feet; no question about that! They are spoiled rotten. There is no hope for animals who are treated like they are. They will think that they can do anything they want. And they probably will be able to, because they will be so friendly with their staff.

My mother warned about this kind of thing. The staff will take advantage of this, she said. They will pick you up and play with you and expect you to like it. A little of that is nice, but I was trained not to do that. I am my own person. It's my nature. I couldn't change if I wanted to.

I hope your literary background includes Rudyard Kipling. I will enlighten those of you who may not be able to read. Some Cats have not had the advantages that I have had. Kipling wrote *The Just So Stories*. He talked about all of the animals, including Cats. He tells that Man invited the Cat into his cave and the Cat said, "I am not a friend, and I am not a servant. I am the Cat who walks by himself, and all places are alike to me."

The Woman made a bargain with him. If she spoke three words in his praise, he could enter the cave, sit by the fire and drink milk. This meant that he would have someplace to go and get fed and be warm.

Baby arrives; Cat amuses Baby, sends him to sleep, and catches a mouse, thus securing the three words of praise. Cat keeps his end of the bargain; he is kind to babies, as long as they don't pull his tail too hard and he keeps the mice down. But when night comes, he is once again the Cat that walks by himself.

I know that I am domesticated and I don't go out at night as many Cats do. But I distance myself from humans, unlike the dog. I am different. I am sorry that Kipling used the tail to show how much we would take. But tail or no tail, I take just so much and then I go my way. I do consider myself a friend to Pollee, but Kipling's story goes a long way toward showing how we Cats think.

Pollee has assured me that she understands. But she says she wouldn't mind if I were a little friendlier to people. I don't know what she means. I greet them at the door. I don't run and hide. I listen to the conversation to make sure they are all right. And I feel I am a great help to Pollee that way. She is alone. Without me, she might let anyone in. Isn't that being friendly?

The next morning, I had planned to eat a bit, although some of it was already eaten, but the ordeal was not over.

As soon as I got up, I went outside. When the humans came home from church, I did not come inside.

Everyone came here to eat-again! And I stayed outside. Finally, Mollie left. I could see her car go. Did she leave those "boys"? I prayed hard that she hadn't, but I had little faith. I was afraid to believe that she had taken them home. Maybe Pollee was going to throw me out and keep them? Surely not!

Finally, it was almost dark and way past my dinner time. But I hadn't been able to eat anyway. I was too upset. Pollee opened the door again and called to me. She had done that repeatedly, but I had ignored her. Well, I had to know. I went in. They were gone!

I couldn't be sure until I searched the house, but they were really gone. And Pollee petted me and my food was there. And everything was as it was before. I was so relieved. I didn't have much faith, I know. I hope I will do better next time.

It has taken me a week to pull myself together and write this. I am not as young as I was and I aged terribly this past week.

Chapter 8

The Canine Conundrum

I guess I must address the subject of dogs. I have no personal animosity toward these animals. They are pets and some people like them. My own people have had dogs. They had what is known as a hunting dog. Apparently he was the best in the world, according to Merritt. At least he talked about his skills all of the time.

I think that dogs have a basic flaw. They feel that they should be trained by their people, whom they think of as their masters, instead of them training the people. This sets a dangerous and foolish precedent. It gives humans the wrong idea of what a pet should be, to start with. And it makes it particularly hard for the rest of us pets.

Cats, on the other hand, see things differently. We are in charge of the home and must spend hours and hours training these humans. This is not always an easy task, faithful reader. In fact, with some people, it is very hard. They never do get it. Think of how much easier it would be if dogs would do it our way and we could all live in harmony.

It's all in the way that dogs perceive themselves. Dogs see themselves as noble beasts who have to work for their keep. They have to guard the house, take care of the children, warn of danger and, if they are the right kind of dog, hunt. They think of their staff as owning them, you know, and this is another big difference.

I do think that all pets should guard their helpers against fires and natural disasters. And you read about both Cats and dogs doing this. It's a natural thing. In return, staff and aides protect their pets from danger.

I read in the Leather Book that salvation is free. We don't have to work for salvation, so why do dogs think they have to work so hard? It's like some people think they have to do things for Jesus in order to be saved. What on earth do they think they could do for God? He owns everything and runs the world, what could I possibly do for Him? I preach for Him and I love Him but I do those things because He loves me and is so good to me. Tabitha, the Cat that lives across the street, is always telling me that she does things for Jesus and He loves her more than me because she does those things. I gave my heart to Him and He can do anything He wants with me, so what I do is love Him and thank Him. Well, I guess we all think a little differently on these things.

I guess the real difference between dogs and Cats is that we Cats have the order right. First come Cats and then the help, in the form of humans. That is the correct order of importance. I'm sure you can see that. We Cats do not have to run around huffing and panting to please our staff. And that is the whole point. We rule quietly and with firmness.

I have a friend named Cindy, who is a dog. She lives with Merritt, the younger, and his family and they think she is wonderful. That's fine. All staff should think their pet is great. She is small, but well, talk about fat; she is bigger than me. In Cindy's defense, both of us like our food and she gets all the table scraps and tidbits from the grandchildren.

For some reason, I get nothing from the table. Just because I have thrown up after trying people food has nothing to do with it, I say. But you know how stubborn humans are. Some things are better left alone with them. Give them their little victories. But, the truth of the matter is that I don't think it looks good for a Cat who can read to consort with a dog. I have to keep up appearances. I hope you don't think that is snobbish. You see, I do have to think of my standing in the pet community.

Occasionally Cindy stays with us. Everyone stays with us. I don't know why I have to put up with that, but I digress. When she stays with us, she wants to make friends, and that would lead to her trying to "play" with me. That means running around and her barking at me and all sorts of undignified things. Cindy is not afraid of me and jumps around to try to get me involved with her silly games. I resist because I know where that would lead. This makes me look unfriendly, but I can't help it.

When Pollee goes to Corrine's house for a Bible Study, I am told that Cindy sits in the same chair with Corrine. Cindy acts as though she is listening and attending the study. Really! Well, maybe she thinks she is doing a cute thing. I hope that is all she thinks. It sounds to me like she is pushing herself forward. My mother says a Cat shouldn't do that. But then, Cindy is a dog. Surprisingly enough, Pollee likes Cindy. Well, no accounting for some people's tastes.

There are two dogs that live next door. They are both pretty foolish dogs and bark a lot. They never help me catch any varmints or help with my study of squirrels but they are pleasant and harmless, for all of their barking. They are good-hearted and leave me alone. And I leave them alone. I don't try to tease them and walk around so that they will bark at me. I have seen Cats do that and it is wrong. It needlessly upsets the dogs and they never seem to understand that most Cats aren't afraid of them, but are only taunting them. Of course, they are fenced in, which I admit is a comfort to me.

I am really quite busy when I am in the yard anyway, and don't have time for endless chatter, as some pets do. I don't mind a pleasant chat with some of the Cats in the neighborhood, and I do like a break from my long days of hard work. I'm afraid that Pollee thinks I am sleeping in the yard, but I am studying the varmints and am using that pose to make them think I am not paying attention. This gives them a false sense of security and I can observe them in their natural habitat.

I think I have made several good points about Cats and dogs, and as long as dogs understand their place in the animal kingdom, I have no quarrel with them.

Chapter 9

Left to My Own Devices

I know that Pollee is going away and I know that she thinks I will miss her. I also know that she has made arrangements with Shirley to feed me. Shirley is a good choice. She does not try to pet me. She does not have much to say and she looks over the yard and sees if there is something she should do. And waters the house plants, too.

Merritt, the younger, would be my first choice, of course. But even if he doesn't feed me he will stop by and see how things are or get a book. He may even turn a light on and stop by after work and turn it off. That is so nice of him. Pollee's kids are nice to her. It's a good thing, too, because they would hear from me if they weren't. I don't care one way or the other about Pollee, but I don't think anyone should mistreat her.

Yes, I see she has the black box filling up. She'll be gone tomorrow, I bet. Then I'll be able to get some much needed rest. I won't have to patrol the yards, since I won't be let out. I have some Cat friends who will do that. They aren't much use, but hopefully, they will come to the patio door and I can give them agreed upon paw instructions. Since Pollee is leaving, I can't get out of the house. Well, they'll just appreciate me more when I resume my work. They know I am an excellent watch-Cat. And everyone needs time off.

Of course, the best part of her vacation is that I won't have to take care of her. Such a relief! You have no idea how much time I spend just keeping her out of trouble. I don't know how she ever managed without me. When Merritt was alive, I did double-duty. He demanded a lot of my time. He expected me to be with him at certain times every day. Fortunately, both of them were pretty predictable and had a schedule, so to speak. That helps a lot when you are expected to wait on them.

Merritt couldn't get through his head the fact that I was a Cat, not a dog. Some dog had certainly spoiled him. It was a bit shocking for me, although I had heard of such things before. He kept talking about Beau, or Show, or was it Moe? Anyway, he never quite got the difference between Cats and dogs.

To add to the confusion, Moe was a hunting dog. That meant that he was Johnny on the Spot all the time. I guess he was always panting around wanting to go hunting or run in the park. Well, I did my best with Merritt. You know the old saying, "You can't teach an old man new tricks." I must say I tried. Pollee was much more pliable because she was so anxious to please.

I imagine I'll get a chance to do some research and study while she's gone. And maybe some light reading. There's enough of that around here. I must say for a Preacher's wife she reads drivel sometimes. Lots of murder mysteries. Tsk..tsk.

DAY ONE. Yes, she's gone. She acted as if I were sorry to see her go. I tried to let her know that I would be fine and didn't care. She doesn't get it. I know she means well, but I am crazy with her fussing. She didn't act like this when Merritt was here. She has changed a bit, I'm afraid. She knows it and seems to think she'll come out of it. I hope so.

DAY TWO. So now I kick back my paws and relax. My mother always said, "Don't let the staff think you are too fond of them. It looks bad to be fawning over them. Let them fawn over you. Play a little hard to get." And that is right. Merritt and Pollee fell in line, very obediently, when they realized that I would not stand for anything less.

Right now, I am concerned because Pollee calls to me in the yard after she eats lunch. "Snickers, do you want to take a nap with me?" Her voice carries and any Cat can hear her. I really would like to rest on her big bed, but I would lose face terribly if I ran in at her beck-and-call.

No, I would like the nap, but as Mother always said, "Keep their minds settled on you, and your problems. This helps bring them out of themselves and takes their mind off their problems. Pets, and especially Cats, are good for people. You hear that all the time. Remember, you are doing them a favor just being in their homes. To take care of a Cat is a privilege."

So how would it look to a listening Cat I had lectured to on not fawning over the staff, if I ran in and obeyed my staff? Can you imagine what "they" would say? The ignominy of it all.

DAY THREE. What a pleasant day to lounge around. Pollee will be home soon. I expect her late Saturday night. It has been a good vacation. I have caught up on my sleep and I'm rarin' to go. I have devised a new way to communicate up and down the block and need to let my fellow Cats know about it.

I've been able to get some writing done. I hope I haven't messed up the computer too badly. But she won't notice. I never did figure out how to get online.

I have done some work. I've kept an eye on the yards. I've patrolled the house carefully. I have not been completely idle. When she comes home, I have to remember to act as if I hardly knew she was gone, but at the same time, act put upon. There is a fine line between the two. I think the last time she went away, I acted a little too happy to have her back. Well, I was glad to see her home safely. And I hear she played Bocce Ball on that trip. So undignified of her, an old lady.

I hope she hasn't been in too much trouble this time.

DAY FOUR. I really think she should be coming home. There are people calling for her. Now, when did she say she would be home?

DAY FIVE. Well, I hissed at Shirley today. I didn't mean to, but *where* is Pollee? Is she lost? Did the plane crash? What is a plane anyway? What will become of me? Did the shuttle man forget her? I am really concerned! Is she in trouble and needing me? It's after 3:00 am.

Wait! I think I hear her. I must act casual. I can greet her at the door, but act as if I didn't know she was gone. She seems to be safe and sound and looking for something to eat. She is talking to me and fussing over me. This is more like it. Now I can get some sleep.

Looking back on this whole adventure, I realize that never once did I put her in Jesus' care. I know from reading the Leather Book that a believer is not supposed to fret and worry. Who could ever do that? I think an exception should be made for me.

I am just a poor, defenseless Cat and I'm sure it's different for me. But I've just read this over and read a bit of the Leather Book again and I guess that Jesus meant it when He said, "Trust and obey." In fact, I was just glancing at the <u>Book of Proverbs</u> and it says, "Trust in the Lord with all of your heart, and lean not unto your own understanding."

Am I wrong again? Isn't there any provision made for poor little Cats like me? How are you supposed to trust when you don't know what is going to happen? Oh, I know. Trust...I guess that's what that means. If I knew what would happen, I wouldn't need trust. Drat! Another thing I've been doing wrong. It's too hard, Lord. Help me! I'm never going to make it.

You know, faithful reader, it has occurred to me that it's not hard if you think of Jesus and who He is and how He wants to help us. I know He is helping me, and maybe some of those bad experiences have a reason. Could this be God's way of teaching me?

Chapter 10

A Near-Death Experience

Well, I really scared that chipmunk. It's time for a nap and then I'll head home. That's what I thought when I got into this cornfield. Now that I'm awake, I'd better get moving. It's probably time to start nagging Pollee to feed me. Let's see. I know it can't be far. I don't remember a cornfield this close to home, though. I'll just start down this corn row. That's funny. This doesn't look familiar. My house should be down there, but it's not. *Where am I?*

Oh, no! I think I'm lost! I'll run over here ...no, there...no... here. Oh, I can't run anymore. What am I going to do? Oh, Lord, help me! I'll never see my home again. I'll never see Pollee again. Oh, Pollee! What will she do without me? She'll never survive.. She needs me. And I need her right now! I'll never be combed by Merritt's old comb again. Oh, the memories! What will become of me? How did I get here?

Wait a minute. I can't panic. I have to think clearly with my keen mind. I know. I'm going to stop and see if I can pray.

"Lord, I am lost. I can't find my way home. I don't know what to do. The Leather Book says that "You never leave one of Yours." I am one of Yours. I decided that when I asked You to save me. I had faith then that You heard me.

"But lately, I haven't been talking to You. I sort of run things by You and figure that I know what to do and You will okay it. I see now that that isn't really praying. I didn't ask if you approved of my plan, I only asked You to bless what I had already decided to do. So, maybe I'm not one of Yours anymore and You have let me go my own way. But I don't know the way! If You are still interested and care though, I sure need You. I am hopelessly lost. I've tried to figure it out, but all these tall corn stalks look alike."

Wait! I know what I need. I need to have faith and trust Him. That seems impossible right now. The stalks are so high, I can hardly see the sun, and the corn is so big and tall. I can't climb the stalks, because they fall under my weight. I tried that. I can't see out. I can only see in the corn row I'm in. And that not too well because it's so dark in here.

Hear my cry, Oh Lord.

All right. I'll quiet down. I'll get a grip on myself. There, I do feel better.

"Lord, I feel as though You heard me! And You did promise. I haven't been a very good Cat. I have been crabby and mean. Oh, Lord, if You rescue me and let me see my home and my staff person, Pollee, again, I'll be nicer to her. And I'll be nice to Emily and Abigail and all of them, even Hannah. And Mollie and Corrine, too. I don't have to be nicer to Merritt, the younger. I already am nice to him. I'll try to be more like You, Jesus. I'll try. I really will. I'll go to Africa to be a missionary if you want me to. I'll give up my bad habits like pestering Pollee all the time. I'll even try to think of others before myself, even though I am very important and can read. I'll work harder on my sermons and my preaching circuit. I'll try to love all the Cats. And even dogs. I'll be kind to dogs, Lord. And I'll be nice to squirrels. Well, You probably don't like squirrels either. But, You might. You're so good, and You sure made a lot of them. Okay, squirrels, too, Lord. Everyone! I'll love everyone. And I'll give You all the credit for saving me, dear Jesus. Please send someone to show me the way home."

I have an idea. Maybe if I could look at the sun, I might be able to figure which way my house faces. But what good would that do? And the sun will be down soon anyway, and it will be cold. I've never gone without my dinner before. Will I die? Or will it take a few days?

Well, I have to find a house with people. And hope that they are nice people. What's the use? I can't see anything but corn. And I can't hear much down here, either. I couldn't even hear if Pollee was calling me with her sweet voice.

Oh, Lord, send someone!

What's that funny noise? Oh, dear. Someone's coming. I'd better hide. They'll hurt me! I'm afraid that I'll never see my home again and some wild creature will eat me.

"What's a matter, kiddo? You in trouble?"

"Don't talk to me, you stupid animal."

Oh, what am I doing? The Lord sent someone to help me and I'm being crabby to him.

But he startled me. He appeared like a bolt out of the blue. Where did he come from? Oh, dear. There's another one. He looks even more frightening. And he came in the same way, suddenly. Where did he come from? Now he will eat me. I don't like funny looking creatures. What kind of animals are they?

"Listen kiddo, I want to help you.."

"Oh, please don't eat me. I'll be nice."

"Aw, lady, I ain't goin' to eat you."

Oh, dear, it's a very large squirrel. I hate squirrels. I'm never nice to them. He'll take me captive and he and his family will have me for dinner. Oh, and the other one's a big rabbit, another one of my enemies. Both of them look different. They have something on their backs.

"Please help me. I don't mean to cry. I'm very brave. No, I'm not. I am scared. I'm lost."

I guess he can't understand me, because I'm crying so hard.

Lord, help me speak clearly so they can understand me. I know you sent this big squirrel and big rabbit to help me.

"Dear Mr. Squirrel and Mr. Rabbit, I am lost. I don't know where my house is."

"Well, why didn't you say so? If you're a city Cat, it's easy to get lost in a big cornfield when the corn is this high. Even a farm Cat would find it easy to get lost in here. Do you live in one of the houses at the end of the street?"

"Yes, I do."

Now I remember. Where the street comes to a dead end, there is a cornfield.

"Yes, sir. If you would be so kind and show me the way out. I suddenly have my wits about me and remember that the sun sets in front of my house. And in the morning, the sun is coming up on my patio. Does that help?"

"Ya, we need to know that because there are houses all around this cornfield. You look pretty frightened and confused. We'll take you to the place where the cornfield ends, with houses facing west."

"Oh, my, you two are so smart. How do you know all of this? Can you read?"

"Lady, we ain't smart wit' books. We're farm pests. We live off the farmers. You must be a city Cat and live off the city people."

"That's right. You probably have heard of me. I'm Snickers, the Preacher Cat, and I can read. I read the Leather Book. You know, about Jesus. You must know Him. I know He sent you."

They looked at each other and sort of smirked.

"You might say we work for Jesus, eh, Bucky?"

Bucky grinned. The squirrel went on: Did you hear that, Bucky? This here Cat is saved. I knew He loved us varmints like squirrels and rabbits, but I guess it's true. He loves all of us, even Cats. You Cats aren't my favorite animals, but you seem nice."

No one ever called me nice before, except Pollee.

"I guess He loves us all. We're His animals."

Bucky nodded.

All this time they had been going down the corn row ahead of me, not too fast, so I could keep up with them. I felt sure they would see we were going in the wrong direction. It felt like that to me. The thought crossed my mind, fleetingly, and was rejected, that they were leading me into a trap, and I would find myself surrounded by big, hostile squirrels and rabbits. I put that thought out of my mind and had faith instead.

Imagine my surprise when we finally came to the end of the row and there, ahead of me was a paved road, my dear, beautiful road. I tried to thank them, but I started crying again, because I was so relieved. They seemed embarrassed.

"Aw, we didn't do nothin'. What were you doing in there, anyhow?"

I started to tell them I was chasing a chipmunk, but my heart was beating so fast I couldn't speak. I couldn't tell them that! I had just told them I was a Christian Cat. What would they think?

The rabbit spoke up. "I bet she was chasing some varmints and they led her into the cornfield so she'd get lost. There are some mean critters out there. They think that's funny. It's a bad thing to do to a nice city Cat like you."

"Oh, sir, I promise I will never follow after an animal, like chasing it, again."

"They run real slow so you'll keep after them till they get you lost. Big Tail and me don't think that's nice, so we keep an eye out for helpless folk like you."

Helpless? I don't like being called helpless. Really! I started to bristle up and then remembered that I WAS helpless and they had saved my life. They were rough creatures, but kind and good. And they said they worked for Jesus. I thanked them properly and from the bottom of my heart.

They were suddenly gone just as a chipmunk appeared. It was the same one who had led me into the cornfield! Now I could get my revenge. I would get him and kill him if it was the last thing I did! I started after him, shouting threats.

And then I realized what I was doing. Just a minute ago, I had promised Jesus I would be good and kind to all, and here I was, doing what I had vowed to never do again. Oh, woe is me! What a miserable creature I am. I can't keep my word for five minutes. And then I thought of Paul. He had said the same thing, although I am sure the circumstances were different. He didn't have murder in his heart. Now Jesus wouldn't have anything to do with me.

Then I remembered about forgiveness. Jesus would forgive me if I admitted my sin. I sure admitted it. I knew it was terrible. So, once again I vowed not to do such things. I wondered how many times I would have to do that? But it felt good and I knew Jesus had heard me.

I am a changed Cat. At least, I hope I am. I try to remember the promises I made Jesus...and there are so many. I don't seem to be doing them all, but I sure do preach better because I know Him better and I know He loves me.

I've never seen Big Tail and Bucky again. They said they work for Jesus. I wonder what they do?

Chapter 11

The Care and Keeping of a Vet

When I look over my eventful life I realize that I have known a great many vets. Vets are part of a Cat's staff, although they don't always seem to understand this. This depends on the vet, of course. And vets judge a Cat on how easy they are to handle. If a Cat shows any independence or spunk, some Vets just think the Cat is difficult, instead of seeing that a spunky Cat is superior to a docile one. In all fairness, I have never had a vet who was mean, even when I was pretty sassy. I want to add this because I don't want to get any vets mad at me, dear reader. That could lead to serious trouble.

On the other hand, to judge a Cat by behavior at the vets isn't always fair. Sometimes we are frightened, so to make a decision about us at this time is a great mistake and a grave misjudgment of character, but it is the easy way out. Maybe I am frightened at the vets. Who wouldn't be? They have a lot of influence with the people who take care of us. To act crabby makes me unpopular, of course, but I have to show them and my owners that I am a force to be reckoned with. Once again, it is hard to be misunderstood, but I have to assert myself. And it has its bright moments, too. It puts a little spice in the trip.

Cindy, the dog at Merritt, the younger's, home, has to have her nails cut at the vets. I heard Abby tell Pollee that Cindy frothed at the mouth, she was so frightened. That's a shame. She probably thinks that the vet is going to cut off her feet, or something. I have heard some tales about vets, but never that they cut off feet. Of course, dogs just aren't real bright sometimes, like we Cats.

One day it began to look as though Pollee and Merritt thought it was time for me to see a vet. When I came to live with Merritt and Pollee, I had a big cage with a faulty door. If I had been given enough time, I could have figured a way to get out of it. But it worried both Merritt and Pollee that I would get out on a busy street or something. As though I wouldn't know how to handle that! So Pollee bought a new cage. She got a smaller one, not pleasing to me. I liked the challenge of the broken door on the old one and it was roomier. Anyway, we Cats distrust new things.

When she bought the cage, she had quite a conversation with the salesman and he told her about a vet in a small town about 10 minutes away. He recommended this man. He also dealt with farm animals. So, it was agreed that they would take me to see this vet.

The day arrived and she got out this tiny cage and I refused to go into it. Merritt was still feeling pretty good at this time and he tried, too. No luck. They decided that they could take me without putting me in the cage if both of them went and Merritt held me in his arms. They optimistically took the cage. I had other plans.

I knew that Merritt would relax his grip and then I would have the freedom of the whole car. Of course, I was right, as usual. When Merritt relaxed his hold, I leaped out of his arms and dashed around the car. I headed for the pedals, got down there, couldn't find anything interesting and finally settled in the backseat. Both of them were very apprehensive and they were right to be. How would they get me into the office? You see, they knew that while I couldn't scratch, I could and would bite.

We arrived. I scrunched down, making it impossible for them to grab me. What a victorious moment. This might sound mean of me, but I have so few victories like this and I was proud of my planning. I might come out and be nice later; I would see.

Pollee went into the office. She came back out and told Merritt that the vet would come out. This sounded like the kind of man I could handle. He was giving in to me.

But when he arrived, I found I was wrong. This was a no-nonsense man. He opened the door of the car, grabbed me gently, but firmly, by the scruff of the neck, like my dear mother used to, and looked me over. I was entranced! He was firm, but kind. I didn't scare him.

He smelled a little like a farm, a good smell, and he gave me the shots. I didn't move. They really don't hurt anyway.

He said, "Do you want her in the cage?"

Pollee and Merritt said, "That would be nice."

I went in without a murmur. I had met my match. He was so commanding and business like that he stole my heart away. I would be pleased to see him again. He had made no comment on my appearance or how I had behaved, but I know he liked me. And, as I say, he was in charge. I had met my master.

I sat quietly and enjoyed the ride on the way home.

I might add that the last time I went out they borrowed Cindy's cage, a much more commodious one. They still had that little one in the basement, but they will never use it. I had made my point.

Chapter 12

Rebellion In the Ranks

It is a sobering thing to have to face betrayal. But that's what it looked like to me. You, dear reader, will find it hard to believe that anyone would want to take over the vast, well organized, well-executed plan I had conceived. But that's what it looked like. I am referring to the neighborhood organization that we call "The Pet Club." I thought that name would disguise our real purpose, which should remain our little secret. No one needed to know that we had a communication system that would be copied and envied by major corporations all over the world if they knew about it. This organization was put together by me when we thought we were facing a dangerous gang of catnappers.

As you remember, gentle reader, I thought that we were all in danger of being kidnapped. I admit I was wrong, but how was I to know that catnapping was not the kidnapping of cats? I told the group at that time that we needed to continue our patrolling to guard against any unknown peril. It was best and would keep us safe from all harm.

But, you know how it goes. As no danger presented itself, the workers began to think that it was unnecessary to spend all that time performing their duties when no one was going to attack us. Complacency entered in and the workers began to relax and neglect their duties. However, it was worse that that.

Not only were the Pets getting slothful about their work, but one, in particular, was heading a rebellion against my leadership. She wanted to take over! I began to suspect this when I heard talk about Tabitha and her cleverness.

"Tabitha says this, and Tabitha says that. Isn't that smart?" The Leather Book says that rebellion is in the heart of man and I was about to find out it is in the hearts of Cats, too.

Tabitha is a scrawny Cat that lives across the street. She has yellow fur. How appropriate for a traitor. She is younger than I, a bit that is, and very talkative and has a way with words. When The Pet Club was begun, by me, I might add, she was all excited. She thought it was great. It enlarged her circle of friends and she said she admired me.

When the group was organized, we met at the garage door. I am speaking of the back door to the garage, which is relatively private. There is a big honeysuckle vine on one side of the door, so the humans wouldn't notice us congregating.

Pollee had remarked to her daughter that she didn't know why I wanted to go into the garage all the time. She finally decided that I was after crickets. I like a snack of a cricket or two, but there is no challenge to hunting them. They can't resist continuing to make that ridiculous noise which leads the hunter right to them. They are crunchy, but those legs are all gristle. But I digress. That wasn't the reason I wanted to go into the garage. I went into the garage for Door Meetings.

Door Meetings are like Cabinet Meetings, but since the only cabinet in the garage is no where near the door, we have Door Meetings. It's not much of a cabinet anyway. I imagine that those big companies and the government have lovely big cabinets.

I wonder how all of those people fit into a cabinet? Humans aren't much for jumping into spaces or sitting on their haunches. Maybe they have benches in the cabinet. It's very puzzling to me. If I were a traveller, I could go and see what they look like but, no matter, we have Door Meetings.

I am the senior Cat. The Cat that lives behind us was here before me, but she does not live on our block. This might be a small point, but Tabitha came here after I did, I'm happy to say, so I not only had the wisdom and brains to think up the plan for The Pet Club; I am the senior Cat.

My Door Members would gather at the back door of the garage, not the noisy door for the car, and we could talk through a very small hole in the rubber on the bottom of the door. I suspect a mouse nibbled the hole there to get in and out. There are no mice in the garage now, of course.

That door cannot be seen from the house. It is very handy. An organization such as we have requires careful planning so that it operates efficiently. And we are forced to be secretive. Cats like to be secretive anyway. Mostly, the animals arrive one by one. And if anyone does see us, they think we are after the pesky mice in the woodpile, which is right by the door. That reminds me, the chipmunks are reproducing at an alarming rate in this neighborhood. It's shocking. They'll soon rival the squirrels. Perish the thought!

Since the murmuring from the group, I have had to spend much more time out in the garage. It is very tiring. I read about murmuring in the Leather Book. A great man named Moses heard a lot of murmuring from a large crowd of rebellious people he was leading around the desert. Such a job! I know just how he must have felt.

Let's get back to the attempted overthrow, or coup, as they say. Coup is a good word to describe this happening, I think. I read it in the dictionary. Looking up words in the dictionary is very difficult for me. First, I have to wait for Pollee to bring the dictionary out. It is in a bookcase with a glass door on it. I just can't get it open. So when Pollee realizes that she must look up a word, I have to grab my chance to look, too. Sometimes she leaves the dictionary out and I can browse. I was browsing when I came across the word coup, and it described my problem to a T, or should I say C? Just thought I would throw a little humor into this sad situation.

One night, Tabitha came over and started talking to me through the window. She has such a loud voice, I could understand her very well. Too well. She said that all the pets wanted a change. We had a very noisy argument and Pollee was surprised. She would have been shocked if she could have understood Cat talk. Tabitha is very mouthy and has quite a vocabulary for a house Cat. If she were a barn Cat, I could understand, but for a Cat who calls herself genteel, well, really!

It wasn't a Cat fight. I don't fight-too risky. I might get hurt. But this does remind me of what Mark Twain said of a Cat fight. "Ignorant people think it is the noise which fighting Cats make that is so aggravating, but it ain't so; it is the sickening grammar that they use." Wasn't he wonderful?

Back to the rebellion. The stories I kept hearing were getting worse and worse. It wasn't just Tabitha that was unhappy. As I mentioned before, a lot of the animals were bored with all the patrolling. They said it wasn't necessary. They hadn't needed it before, and after all, I had been wrong about the catnapping. I felt that we still needed to be on our guard, and I realized we couldn't just let it go.

I was watching the birds one day and noticed how they alerted each other to danger, and how well it worked. When I go out sometimes, I hear the noise and realize that there must be a bird near me, maybe a baby bird, and some Good Samaritan is warning that bird that I am outdoors. Bird and Cats are not what you would call "friendly," but maybe trying to get them to help with our watch would be a good thing.

I finally managed to get close enough to a bird to have a conversation. They are very leery of Cats, and I guess you could say, rightly so. But this Blue Jay was a bit bold and brassy. Aren't all Blue Jays that way? They are really mouthy, but I digress again. I made my proposal to him, asking for them to cooperate with us. He was surprisingly agreeable. He agreed to tell the other birds and they would warn us with loud chirps and screeches. We both agreed that would also alert the predators, but might scare them off, too.

I knew I couldn't let my disgust for Tabitha keep me from protecting my fellow pets. I learned in the Leather Book to pray for our enemies, and I guess protecting them falls into that category. We have to band together, friends and enemies, against the bullies and bad guys.

It wasn't long after that, that it happened. Pollee was in the bedroom and glanced out the window and gasped. There was a falcon, or what looked like one. Maybe it was a small hawk. It was at least 12-inches tall. That's a big bird! She got out the bird book and looked for it. The bird, or whatever it was, just sat there under the tree outside the window. It looked as dignified as an owl. Maybe it *was* an owl.

Pollee's first concern was for her beloved Cat, me. She called the vet. The lady there said, "Yes, that could be a hawk."

Pollee asked, "Could a hawk pick up a 12-pound Cat?"

The lady said, "Yes."

That meant that a lot of animals, including me, could be whisked away. Thus ended my freedom to go out for awhile, because Pollee thought I would be carried away. But I needed to warn everybody, and she would still let me out into the garage. I called a Door Meeting. Thank goodness we still had the patrol. We got busy and every pet in the neighborhood knew about that bird in a few minutes. We would be on our guard and watch. If we saw it coming, we would go to some kind of shelter, like a patch of flowers or better yet, a bush. We could be safe there.

Pollee thought maybe that bird was a trained falcon. It was sitting under a tree, close to the house, and stayed there for some time and didn't seem frightened. Very strange.

We never learned what it was or where it came from, but it saved The Pet Club. I don't think it just happened. I think that Jesus sent that bird to show the Pet Club how much it was needed. I thanked Him for it.

I wish I could plan a party for us all. But then everyone would know we were organized and all our staff wouldn't understand, and would try to stop it, probably. They don't understand much. I have to smile at Pollee and the things she says and does. After she has been out and I greet her at the door, she will say, "Snickers, I'm sorry I've been gone so long. Did you miss me?"

I'll say, "Not really, I can amuse myself, you know."

But she doesn't know. Sometimes, I would like to be able to hold a real conversation with her. She would be amazed at my clever and deep thoughts.

Chapter 13

A Murder on the Patio

First, I want to say that I am innocent of any wrong doing in the death of that bird. I was not present when the altercation, or whatever it was, took place. In fact, I don't know what happened. When I returned to the patio after I had reconnoitered around the house, as was my fashion, there was a dead bird, not a sparrow, thank goodness.

The sparrow is mentioned in the Leather Book and I don't ever want to mess with a sparrow. Jesus said He sees when a sparrow falls, so I know they are special. I am always nice to them. What's so special about them, I can't see, but I am not going to pick a quarrel with them.

To get back to the story, apparently there was a fight. There were feathers all over the place. It was a mess. Pollee came out and swept the evidence away and put the bird in the garden-swept him in, I should say. She is a heartless woman sometimes. What if I had left that bird there as a present for her? What thanks did I get? But, I repeat, I did not do it.

Since I made friends with that Blue Jay, I would never kill a bird. We need the birds in the Pet Club. We need all the allies we can get. Since birds are a bit scatter-brained and not too bright, I don't want to confuse them by asking for their help and then killing one of them, although they can be a bother to me.

The birds were all gone and have been very quiet. When I finally saw one, I offered to hold an inquiry about this death, but they act funny, which makes me think that I am automatically the guilty party in their eyes.

The bird who was killed, was a big one, the size of a grackle, I would say, or dove, but it is not a grackle or dove. I stay away from birds that big. I have seen them fighting among themselves and it's not pretty. One of them will pick on their fellow grackle, let's say. They both look the same to me; same size and everything, but one considers himself better than the other. Birds tend to look alike, I have observed. But the one bird will peck at the other and not let him eat with him. Seems very unfriendly to me.

I admit I try to keep the birds away. They are a messy bunch, but I have not attacked one bird. In reality, they are very fast and can always fly away if you get close. I have seen some cats creep up to a bird and catch it, but I have not had much success doing that. I have seen what happens sometimes to Cats when they try that. Sometimes the birds gang up and it is frightening what they can do. Anyway, I said I would serve as the judge in the matter of the bird incident, but they walk or fly away when I suggest it. I have to admit this incident certainly cleared the birds away from the patio better than I've ever been able to do.

I think, for it to be murder, it would have to be another bird who did the deed. I'm not certain of the birds' laws. Birds keep themselves to themselves. But I think a bird could plead self-defense or accidental death. As I said, though, I've seen birds be pretty aggressive to each other.

As usual, my counsel was not sought, although I am the most educated of all of these creatures, I assure you. Probably the best thing to do is to let the subject drop. But I repeat to anyone who will listen, I am innocent. I am a peace-loving Cat and highly regarded in the Cat community. I can provide character references.

Although I am not what would be called a "friend" of birds, I am not a killer, either. I just kill mice, which is legal for a Cat, you know. We are expected to do that. I know that in some circles, it is thought that we Cats kill birds, too. I see nothing wrong with that, but they are big, and not very tasty. And very hard to catch, as well. They are crafty. Any group that relies on its good looks the way birds do, and for handouts, too, is bound to be shifty and lazy. That's what Mother always said and Mother was always right.

You have heard the expression, a "wise old bird." I have seen very few wise old birds. They are very excitable, always following a leader, who may not know any more than they do. Seems to me they are a lot like people. No offense meant, but I am sure you know what I mean. You've seen that, everyone following a human who knows nothing, or worse, is leading these people away for gain for himself. You have seen that happen, I'm sure. I hope you have never done that. Especially if you are an adult person. Very foolish and can lead to great hardship and suffering. That's what the Leather Book says, too.

I will say one thing for birds. They never interbreed. They keep their blood lines clean. And, although I have seen different breeds of birds socialize, when the party is over, they go their own ways. I'm not sure that is altogether a good thing. Some varieties are superior to others and a little mixing of the genes might be a help.

I like to think on these deep subjects. It keeps me studying and enlarges the boundaries of the mind, so to speak. I have often thought I would like to sit in on classes at college, accounting a class, I think they call it. Or is it auditing? Some word like that. I'm sure I would be a great contributor, but they would not be able to communicate with me.

My language is far more complicated than any human realizes. Manx are especially gifted in that area. We have a great variety of sounds, mews, or chirps, as they call it. Maybe I could teach some other Manx's to read. I wonder if I could teach Domino to read? He seemed like a bright fellow and Mollie says he is very wise, for a teenager. I will mull that over in my mind.

The Cat I taught to read would have to live here with me. No, on second thought, I am much too busy to have another Cat in the house, and I don't feel like sharing Pollee. She has her hands full with me. I can keep her busy. But wait! I could have Door Meetings! You know, over by the door. I know there are enough Leather Books around here to supply several Cats. Well, another subject to ponder and I'm busy as it is. Such is the life of a Cat with a great mind.

Chapter 14

A Space of My Own

Sometimes I yearn for a space of my own. I know I have the lower level and it is fine for reading. Most of the preacher books are down there and I like to curl up with a good book. But it isn't private and I have to watch and listen for Pollee clunking downstairs.

I think that I could fix up a space of my own in the garage that would do very nicely. I could sneak the Leather Book out and I would like a CD Player so that I could listen to CDs. Merritt, the younger, records his sermons on CDs and I would like to listen and maybe get some ideas for my sermons. I still haven't had much luck with the Cats around here. They are tough customers when it comes to receiving the Word.

I could have regular hours for Cats to call. Maybe I could serve tea at certain hours. It would be catnip tea, but I would limit my friends' consumption. I wouldn't want them out on the street feeling a little tipsy. That could be dangerous on top of all the other hazards that Cats face every day.

I always have wanted to be able to keep records of the activities of the Pet Club. And if I had a space of my own I could have a filing cabinet for keeping those records and important papers, too. The possibilities are endless. Maybe even a desk. No, that wouldn't be necessary and it might be a little obvious.

When we had our Door Meetings, I would be there and not have to count on Pollee being home to let me out. Or if she had called me in, I could signal from the patio door to postpone the meeting and set another time. Cats are a bit casual about meetings since they have to rely on their staff to let them in and out. A Cat door would be nice, but not many owners have that.

I would like to address Cat's aides at this time. I believe you picked up this little book hoping to understand your Cat better. Understanding will make you a better aide to your Cat. That's something we all want. I think it would be informative and helpful if you read this book aloud to your Cat. We are in this together, Cat lovers. I call you all Cat lovers because most people are, although they may not realize it.

I also suggest that you leave your books accessible to your Cats. And if you don't have a Leather Book, get one. It will be good for you, too. Many people have learned to read with the Leather Book. Remember that's what happened to me. A well-read Cat is a happy Cat, and isn't that your goal? It might make my efforts to reach all Cats with the Gospel easier, too.

I guess another reason I would like a space of my own is to meditate. For example, I have been pondering a lot lately about humans' obsession with leaves. It's fall here and everyone is out in the cold taking care of the leaves that have fallen from their trees.

Have you noticed how much time humans spend gathering up leaves? It's a lot of work. They use a rake and gather the leaves in bags. Or they might put them in a barrel, or something. The people that mow them put them in a bag attached to the lawn-mowing machine. They take great care to get each and every leaf. Once they get them, they carefully put them in the containers and put the lid on, too. They don't want to lose any. And as soon as they finish, they start again. After that, they put the containers full of leaves out in front and a big truck comes and collects them.

I think I have finally figured out why they do all this work. I believe that the leaves are very valuable and they get money for them. They probably get a check in the mail. It's a cash crop, like tobacco used to be. Maybe it still is. But what are the leaves good for? What possible use could they have?

I once heard Pollee and Merritt telling someone about the people on Prince Edward Island, which is somewhere up north where they visited. These people would go out with carts and collect seaweed from the Atlantic Ocean that washed up on the beach certain times of the year. It was sold to some company that said it was used for medicine. It sounds fishy and far fetched to me, but they swore it was true.

Could the folks around here be using old dead leaves for something like that? That's preposterous. Or is it? All of the workers seem so serious about it. They must be making pretty good money from doing this.

Surely it isn't used to make drugs! But what else would pay so well to make them work that hard? These people use all their spare time gathering those leaves. I guess they have to harvest them all at once so they won't spoil. You can see that I have given the matter a great deal of thought. If I ever find out the truth about the matter, I will let you know at once.

This will give you an idea of the kind of thing I think about. I get into my bowl and think. My bowl is similar to the ones they have in Washington, D.C. They call them think-tanks, but they must be bowls; a tank would be so uncomfortable, and might be hard to breathe in, too.

Now you can see the importance of my having a space of my own. Not only would I enjoy it, but I might solve quite a few of the world's problems, too. You see, dear reader, I'm not just thinking of myself. I am a very unselfish Cat. Most of us are.

Chapter 15

All Good Things Must Come to an End

I have discovered that I might, just might, have made a mistake using the garage as a space of my own. As I journey through this vale of tears, I do have a few regrets. Well, it hasn't been a vale of tears for me, because Cats don't cry tears. But I must admit that even I have made a few, not many, but a few, mistakes. And one of them was moving into the garage hoping to make a space of my own.

It doesn't look like it will work out. There are a few flaws in the plan. The first problem is that I don't have access to watching Pollee as she should be watched, and when she is not watched, she gets into trouble. She needs constant care and if someone came to the door, I would never know, and it is important for me to know. She could let the wrong sort of person in or do something else foolish.

If I am there to demand time and attention, it gets her out of her comfort zone and up on her feet. Older people need to move around. It's good for them. That's probably why Cats are so good for an old person. There

I go again, always thinking of others. I am a wonderful companion for her. Well, I would be for anyone. Cats who just sit around on their staffs' laps are encouraging their staff to be slothful. And Sloth is one of the seven deadly sins. I'm always trying to save Pollee from herself.

The second problem with the garage involves the neighborhood Cats. I no sooner get settled in the think-bowl with a weighty problem to solve, than someone mews at the door. I feel I must answer because I never know if an emergency has arisen and I am the only Cat who can handle it. Being in charge is a big responsibility, but a good leader does not shirk duty.

So, I get up and go to the door and let my neighbor in. Then I find out that this Cat only wants to chat and expects a cup of catnip tea with the conversation. They don't seem to understand when I explain that I am busy. As far as they are concerned, I am only sitting in the bowl. They are so inconsiderate. How do they think I got so smart? I've had to think a great deal and it is heavy on my brain sometimes. I hate to strain my wonderful brain. So this is what happens to my afternoon to think. It's gone before I know it. You, dear reader, can see that this is a major problem.

But that's not all. I can't get out of the garage so I miss what is going on in the yards. Another problem is the heat and cold. The garage is not air conditioned, nor heated. What an oversight on Pollee's part. But that is the case. I do have a beautiful coat like no one else; but nevertheless, when one is thinking, one needs to be able to concentrate and not be bothered by all of these distractions.

There is also the problem of the Door Meetings. Cats think they can have one any time. They think they are there, so let's have a Door Meeting. That won't work. So, we will go back to handling them the way we did before. A Door meeting will be regularly scheduled and be part of the neighborhood bark, and that can call the Cats together. That way, Cats won't show up any old time, interrupt me and demand a Door Meeting.

So, I have taken the file cabinet and the think-bowl back in the house. I have put them down in the lower level. I have more privacy there than I do in the garage. As Robert Burns once said, "The best laid schemes o' mice and men gang aft agley."

Now why do they say mice? Mice are good planners, but not as clever at it as we Cats. But no matter. Some of these sayings are a little strange. And he did write this a long time ago, and with a Scottish spelling. He probably got it wrong. The saying most likely started out as Cats and men. On the other hand, Cats' plans generally do work out because we are so clever.

Back to the garage: it just doesn't have the amenities that I am accustomed to. I thought I could overlook these little details, but my sensitive nature can't. I guess I could look around for a good Cat Decorator. I know there is one in town.

Pollee may not see eye-to-eye with me on this issue. She doesn't even know I am using the garage for my office. She misses a lot, because she is not very observant, and, as I have said before, she is old.

It will be easier to go back to using the Lower Level. I will miss the Cat visitors, but not that much. They really aren't my intellectual equals. It would be hard to find many Cats that are.

I do like the car in the garage. It is a touch of class even though it isn't a brand new model. Sometimes after Pollee has used it, it is still warm. That's cozy. And if it has been raining, it's wonderful. I get really fresh water that way. And an occasional drink of snow water is good. I have very simple tastes for a Cat of my caliber.

So, back to the think-tank, but in the lower level. I know, it's the basement, but don't you think "lower level" sounds a little classier? I do have a real problem to ponder. How can I help Pollee when she leaves the house? Who knows what trouble she gets into? I wonder. For example, she tells me she is going shopping. I assume that means going to a store and buying something.

It is interesting when she comes home with food. That's shopping. But it also means that she has bought things and made decisions without me. I hate that. Shopping for clothes is another matter. I will say that one clothing store she goes to has great crinkly paper bags. They make lots of noise when I get into them, and they are perfect for a nice nap, and being paper I have no fear about smothering. Pollee puts the bag on the living room floor and I can get into it and feel safe. That way I still have an eye on things but people don't notice me.

Sometimes she says she is going shopping, but doesn't come home when I think she should. When she does come home, she says she couldn't find anything. How strange. Did she get lost? Were the shops closed? Has she been gone for hours and searching for a store all that time? Was she wandering around in a daze? Did they move the shops around? Apparently not. She doesn't seem to be too upset when that happens.

Sometimes, she will be talking to someone about a store and she will say they don't have anything. Now there's a puzzlement. If they don't have anything, why are they called a store? That's when I head for the bowl.

Sometimes, she goes out to lunch with friends. I wouldn't go out to lunch, not even with friends. They might decide they liked my lunch better than theirs and eat it. And I wouldn't invite people to come here to the house to eat like she does, either. Eating is serious business. I want to eat by myself, at the same place, the same time, or earlier, and I don't want to share with some other Cat. Also, I don't do something else while I eat, like talking. Eating is important and I give all my attention to it.

Speaking of eating, I play a little game with Pollee. I try to get her to feed me earlier every day. I win often. At first, she would feed me at 6:00 pm and now I generally can get fed by 3:15. Not bad, eh? I get her to feed me earlier by sitting and looking at her and mewing softly. Then, if she doesn't respond, I sit with my back to her. That is a real put-down for a person. When a Cat does that, they are really displeased with you.

I don't ask her to feed me in the morning and I never wake her up. She doesn't have her wits about her at any time, but the morning is especially bad. So my dinner time is late in the day. You may think these details are unimportant, but they are fascinating to me.

I think I need to present an apologetic for some people being crabby. An apologetic in Christian circles is a defense of Christianity and why we should believe what the Leather Book says. I am preparing an apologetic for temperamentally challenged Cats.

Because I am so clever, and know how to read, I can read you know, I should not be held to the same standards as ordinary people. I should be allowed to be crabby because I am a little different than a lot of people. Hmm. That doesn't sound right, somehow. I'll put that on the agenda for the think-bowl.

Anyway, I am a bit short-tempered on occasions, mostly because I have a lot on my mind. It's nothing personal. My heroine is Lucy Van Pelt. There is a girl who has things together, as they say. I hope you remember her. She was in the Charles Schulz comic strip, *Peanuts*. That was a wonderful comic strip. Some people don't like Lucy because she is mean to Charlie Brown. I do like Charlie Brown and I don't like him being picked on and I don't do that myself. But after all, Lucy isn't perfect. She is very crabby and very clever. She is the one who said that the world needs crabby people. And that is exactly the way I feel. Things would be pretty slipshod if it weren't for crabby people. Being nice is important for Pollee and other staffers, but these nice people need guidance or they let things go, under the guise of being nice.

If there were no crabby people-or let me put it this way; if there were no particular people, who would be in charge? I know, you are saying that it is possible to be particular and nice, too. I say no. In order to motivate many people, they need a firm hand and sometimes that means being crabby.

I've heard it said that some people are just crabby for no reason at all. They don't care how things are done. They are just plain crabby. Those people are not entitled to be crabby; only those of us who are trying to make things better can be crabby.

Pollee says that as a Christian, I should be kind. I am kind-every once in awhile. If I were not crabby, staffers and relatives of staffers would think they could pick me up and hold me on their laps. How undignified. If you dispense favors, the aides grow lax and things don't get done. I've seen it happen. Crabby people are misunderstood. We are a dying breed. We have standards and expect a certain kind of behavior from those around us. I don't mean to say that there is a shortage of crabby people. We can always be found, but I'm speaking of particular crabby people.

What the world needs is more servants. I could keep a few busy and then I could get more done. I'm always ready for a nap because I work so hard. But a Cat's work is never done. That's an old saying that has been changed. Nowadays, they say a woman's work is never done, but we Cats know it started out as "a Cat's work is never done."

Remember, when the vermin mice take over a building, whom do they call? Cats! No one else can do the job like we do. If you put poison down, the vermin die any old place and then the odors are terrible. But we Cats get rid of them and even bring them to our humans. We do the job right. Ask any sailor whom they need on board their ships. They will immediately tell you the three "C's': a captain, and cook and Cats.

I must tell you, dear reader, that I am almost through with this book. It has been a real challenge for me, but I am glad that I had the chance to write it. These things I have told you need to be known. But I am tired and need to have this great responsibility lifted from my shoulders. You know the Leather Book says in *Ecclesiastes* that "In the making of many books there is no end, and much study wearies the body." I think I can take that to mean chapters, as well as books.

Mark Twain says about the same thing in his book, *Huckleberry Finn*. Huck says, "There is nothing more to write about and I am rotten glad, because if I had known what trouble it was to make a book I wouldn't have tackled it and I ain't going to do it no more." I know what he means. It has taken a WHOLE LOT OF WORK!

I am tired and I feel I have given you a lot to ponder. I am finished, and I think that the things I have told you are important to everyone, even those of you that aren't Cat helpers. So, I bid farewell, faithful readers, until we meet again.

Epilogue

Laughter Brings Healing Through a Cat

There we were sitting around the table, laughing and telling funny stories about Merritt, my husband, their father, father in law and grandpa. The stories warmed our hearts and the laughter was a tonic.

Merritt had preached for most of his life and was good at what he did. He was well-liked wherever he went, in and out of church. He had died about a month before and we were all still coping with our personal grief. There had always been a lot of laughing when Merritt was around, and we were determined to continue doing and saying things that would keep that laughter with us.

There had not been the shock of sudden death. Merritt had been ill and dying for too long. We knew he loved the Lord and was with Him. He was 84 when he died. But it still hurt.

The conversation turned to Snickers. Snickers was the cat that Merritt and I had decided to get after our last dog had died. We felt that a cat would be less maintenance for us in our senior years. We saw an ad...Manx-type female, calico markings...needs a home because of impending move. It sounded like what we wanted.

She was a beautiful cat, no question about that. But she was temperamentally-challenged, I always said. The family said she was crabby. Once, Hannah, the oldest granddaughter, 16 at the time, had been hired to feed her when we went on a trip. Snickers apparently wasn't happy with this situation. We said she probably missed us. Hannah said she was biting the hand that fed her.

Admittedly, Snickers was not what you would ever call a friendly cat. She was kind of friendly to Merritt and me. Well, I have to admit 'friendly' wasn't exactly the word. I guess it would be more accurate to say she tolerated us.

So, sometimes at those Sunday after-church family get-togethers after Merritt's death, the topic would be Snicker's latest insulting behavior. I would explain that she was frightened and felt that a good offense was better than a poor defense. She had watched a lot of football with Merritt. When I used that as an explanation for her irritability, they really laughed.

I felt that Snickers needed someone to defend her from these verbal attacks, so, the next Sunday I was prepared. I had written, well, Snickers had written a defense of her behavior. Her excuses and reasoning were a bit faulty. In fact, they were so off base that we were all laughing.

Next Sunday, I had another defense of her poor behavior. Snickers took over and was soon explaining how she had learned to read because Merritt had left Bibles open all over the house. Merritt was a preacher, and furthermore, she said that I couldn't get him to pick them up and put them away. I wasn't forceful enough.

But my behavior had helped her teach herself to read. Another helpful thing was our habit of reading out loud, Scripture and other interesting things, to each other. Snickers would position herself on the reader's chair so she could see and hear the passages being read. She reported that in no time at all, she was reading.

After Merritt died, Snickers, being the kind and thoughtful cat she was, decided to write a book to be used as a training manual to help "cat staffers". Snickers never referred to staffers and aides as owners. She said that was very demeaning to cats. I found that she led another life outside the home, full of danger and exciting exploits, showing her leadership qualities among the pets in the area. Could all of this be true?

It was understood that I should carefully read this book, which was blatantly directed at me. She explained that she was to write the book, and I was to get it published. Since I never expected the book to get done, I casually agreed.

One day, I asked a friend of mine if she wanted to read a chapter. When she returned it, she said, "This must have been great therapy for you." I was stunned. It had been great therapy for me, and also to my family.

About a year after Merritt died, Snickers announced that the book was finished. A few months later, at the age of ten, Snickers unexpectedly died. She had accomplished what the Lord had sent her to do.... to see us through a hard time.

As I look back, I am so grateful the Lord sent this cat to help me. It has been a comforting thing to once again be reminded of how Jesus cares for us. The fact that we answered that ad and took Snickers home was part of God's Plan to give me comfort. When her work was done, she moved on, mission accomplished. Is this a silly idea? Maybe so, but it warmed my heart and helped me heal.

Do I believe that a cat could write a book? No.

Do I believe that a cat could inspire me to write a book? Yes

Do I believe that God knew that I would need this cat and sent her ahead? Yes!

A cat came to stay with us and that made all the difference.